William Maxwell

SO LONG, SEE YOU TOMORROW

William Maxwell was born in 1908, in Lincoln, Illinois. When he was fourteen his family moved to Chicago. He continued his education there and at the University of Illinois. After a year of graduate work at Harvard he went back to Urbana and taught freshman composition, and then turned to writing. He has published six novels, three collections of short fiction, an autobiographical memoir, a collection of literary essays and reviews, and a book for children. For forty years he was a fiction editor at *The New Yorker*. From 1969 to 1972 he was president of the National Institute of Arts and Letters. He has received the Brandeis Creative Arts Award Medal and, for *So Long, See You Tomorrow*, the American Book Award and the Howells Medal of the American Academy of Arts and Letters. He lives with his wife in New York City.

INTERNATIONAL

SO LONG,
SEE YOU
TOMORROW

William Maxwell

VINTAGE INTERNATIONAL

Vintage Books

A Division of Random House, Inc.

New York

For Robert Fitzgerald

SO LONG,
SEE YOU
TOMORROW

I

A Pistol Shot

The gravel pit was about a mile east of town, and the size of a small lake, and so deep that boys under sixteen were forbidden by their parents to swim there. I knew it only by hearsay. It had no bottom, people said, and because I was very much interested in the idea that if you dug a hole straight down anywhere and kept on digging it would come out in China, I took this to be a literal statement of fact.

One winter morning shortly before daybreak, three men loading gravel there heard what sounded like a pistol shot. Or, they agreed, it could have been a car backfiring. Within a few seconds it had grown light. No one came to the pit through the field that lay alongside it, and they didn't see anyone walking on the road. The sound was not a car backfiring; a tenant farmer named Lloyd Wilson had just been shot and killed, and what they heard was the gun that killed him.

At the coroner's inquest, Wilson's uncle, who had lived with him for a number of years and was a man in his late sixties, testified that while he was feeding the horses he saw his nephew's lantern as he passed on his way to the cow barn. The horse barn and the cow barn were about five hundred feet apart. He did not hear the shot and he was not aware that there was anybody on the farm that morning who did not belong there. The household at that time consisted of Wilson, his two little boys, aged six and nine, his elderly housekeeper, and the uncle, Fred Wilson.

The housekeeper then took the stand and testified that on the last morning of his life Lloyd Wilson got up at five-thirty as usual, dressed, and built two fires. While he was waiting for the one in the kitchen range to catch, he stood talking and joking with her. He was in a cheerful mood and left the house whistling. Usually he was through milking and back in the kitchen before she had breakfast ready. At seven o'clock, knowing that he had to go to town and pick up a man he had engaged to do some belated corn shucking for him, she told the younger of the two little boys to go see what was keeping his father so long. He asked for a flashlight, and she peered out into the darkness and then said he didn't need a flashlight, he could see the lantern shining from the open door of the barn. In a very short while she heard him coming back to the house. He was crying. When she opened the storm door and called out to him, he said, "Papa is dead! He is sitting there with his eyes open but he is dead. . . ."

Who believes children. Brushing him and his story aside she ran to the barn. Wilson was sitting on a milking stool in the middle stall, his body sunk over against the partition. She caught him by the hand and cried, "Lloyd, what on earth is the matter with you?"—thinking he had been stricken with heart failure or possibly apoplexy. As the child had said, he was sitting there with his eyes open but he was dead.

The housekeeper and Fred Wilson did the necessary things —that is to say, she went back to the house and made a number of telephone calls, and he finished milking the cows and turned them out into the pasture and then sat beside the body until the undertaker and his assistant came and took it back to town. Rigor mortis had set in, and they had to cut the sleeve of his jacket in order to take off his clothes. They removed the jacket, coat, corduroy vest, and flannel shirt, before they saw a small red stain on the undershirt, over the heart.

In those days—I am talking about the early nineteen-twenties—people in Lincoln mostly didn't lock their doors at night, and if they did it was against the idea of a burglar. One sometimes read in the evening paper that some man had been arrested for disorderly conduct, but that meant drunkenness. Without thinking I would have said that acts of violence could hardly be expected to flourish in a place where the houses were not widely separated and never enclosed by a high wall and where it would have been hard to do anything out of the way that somebody by one accident or another or from simple curiosity would not happen to see. But consider the following sentence, from a history of Logan County published in 1911: "While there have been in the neighborhood of about fifty fatal shooting affrays . . . very few have occurred where the parties were well known or of considerable standing in the community." As a rule the shooting, or the knifing, or the clubbing, was in a coal miner's shack or a back alley or a lonely farmhouse, but one of the crimes mentioned in that book took place in a house on Tenth Street, one street over from the house we lived in when I was a child. What distinguished the murder of Lloyd Wilson from all the others was a fact so shocking that the Lincoln *Courier-Herald* hesitated several days before printing it: The murderer had cut off the dead man's ear with a razor and carried it away with him. In that pre-Freudian era people did not ask themselves what the ear might be a substitution for, but merely shuddered.

2

The Period of Mourning

I very much doubt that I would have remembered for more
than fifty years the murder of a tenant farmer I never laid
eyes on if (1) the murderer hadn't been the father of somebody I knew, and (2) I hadn't later on done something I was
ashamed of afterward. This memoir—if that's the right name
for it—is a roundabout, futile way of making amends.

Before I can go into all that, I have to take up another
subject. When my father was getting along in years and the
past began to figure more in his conversation, I asked him
one day what my mother was like. I knew what she was like
as my mother but I thought it was time somebody told me
what she was like as a person. To my surprise he said,
"That's water over the dam," shutting me up but also leaving me in doubt, because of his abrupt tone of voice, whether
he didn't after all this time have any feeling about her much,
or did have but didn't think he ought to. In any case he
didn't feel like talking about her to me.

Very few families escape disasters of one kind or another, but in the years between 1909 and 1919 my mother's
family had more than its share of them. My grandfather,
spending the night in a farmhouse, was bitten on the ear by
a rat or a ferret and died three months later of blood poi-

soning. My mother's only brother was in an automobile accident and lost his right arm. My mother's younger sister poured kerosene on a grate fire that wouldn't burn and set fire to her clothing and bore the scars of this all the rest of her life. My older brother, when he was five years old, got his foot caught in a turning carriage wheel.

I was so small when these things happened that either I did not know about them or else I didn't feel them because they took place at one remove, so to speak. When my brother undressed at night he left his artificial leg leaning against a chair. It was as familiar to me, since we slept in the same room, as his cap or his baseball glove. He was not given to feeling sorry for himself, and older people were always careful not to show their sorrow over what had happened to him. What I felt about his "affliction" was tucked away in my unconscious mind (assuming there is such a thing) where I couldn't get at it.

My younger brother was born on New Year's Day, at the height of the influenza epidemic of 1918. My mother died two days later of double pneumonia. After that, there were no more disasters. The worst that could happen had happened, and the shine went out of everything. Disbelieving, we endured the wreath on the door, and the undertaker coming and going, the influx of food, the overpowering odor of white flowers, and all the rest of it, including the first of a series of housekeepers, who took care of the baby and sat in my mother's place at mealtime. Looking back I think it more than likely that long before she ever laid eyes on us that sallow-faced, flat-chested woman had got the short end of the stick. She came from a world we knew nothing about, and I don't remember that she ever had any days off. She may have made a stab at being a mother to my older brother and me, but it would have taken a good deal more than that to break through our resistance. We knew what we had had, and were not going to be taken in by any form of counterfeit affection.

My mother's sisters and my father's sisters and my grandmother all watched over us. If they hadn't, I don't know what would have become of us, in that sad house, where nothing ever changed, where life had come to a standstill. My father was all but undone by my mother's death. In the evening after supper he walked the floor and I walked with him, with my arm around his waist. I was ten years old. He would walk from the living room into the front hall, then, turning, past the grandfather's clock and on into the library, and from the library into the living room. Or he would walk from the library into the dining room and then into the living room by another doorway, and back to the front hall. Because he didn't say anything, I didn't either. I only tried to sense, as he was about to turn, which room he was going to next so we wouldn't bump into each other. His eyes were focused on things not in those rooms, and his face was the color of ashes. From conversations that had taken place in front of me I knew he was tormented by the belief that he was responsible for what had happened. If he had only taken this or that precaution . . . It wasn't true, any of it. At a time when the epidemic was raging and people were told to avoid crowds, he and my mother got on a crowded train in order to go to Bloomington, thirty miles away, where the hospital facilities were better than in Lincoln. But even if she had had the baby at home, she still would have caught the flu. My older brother or my father or I would have given it to her. We all came down with it.

I had to guess what my older brother was thinking. It was not something he cared to share with me. I studied the look in his hazel eyes and was startled: If I hadn't known, I would have thought that he'd had his feelings hurt by something he was too proud to talk about. It was the most he could manage in the way of concealment. At night we undressed and got into bed and fell asleep without taking advantage of the dark to unburden our hearts to each other. It strikes me as strange now. It didn't then. Though we were very different, he knew me inside out—that is to say, he knew my weaknesses and how to play on them, and this had made me leery about exposing my feelings to him. I also suspect that I had told on him once too often. I have no way of knowing what he might have said. What I didn't say, across the few feet that separated our two beds, was that I couldn't understand how it had happened to us. It seemed like a mistake. And mistakes ought to be rectified, only this one couldn't be. Between the way things used to be and the way they were now was a void that couldn't be crossed. I had to find an explanation other than the real one, which was that we were no more immune to misfortune than anybody else, and the idea that kept recurring to me, perhaps because of that pacing the floor with my father, was that I had inadvertently walked through a door that I shouldn't have gone through and couldn't get back to the place I hadn't meant to leave. Actually, it was the other way round: I hadn't gone anywhere and nothing was changed, so far as the roof over our heads was concerned, it was just that she was in the cemetery.

When I got home from school I did what I had always done, which was to read, curled up in the window seat in the library or lying flat on my back on the floor with my feet in a chair, in the darkest corner I could find. The house was full of places to read that fitted me like a glove, and I read the same books over and over. Children tend to derive comfort and support from the totally familiar—an umbrella stand, a glass ashtray backed with brightly colored cigar bands, the fire tongs, anything. With the help of these and

other commonplace objects—with the help also of the two
big elm trees that shaded the house from the heat of the sun,
and the trumpet vine by the back door, and the white lilac
bush by the dining-room window, and the comfortable
wicker porch furniture and the porch swing that contributed
its *creak . . . creak . . .* to the sounds of the summer night
—I got from one day to the next.

My father got from one day to the next by attending
faithfully to his job. He was the state agent for a small fire
insurance company and traveled from one end of Illinois to
the other, inspecting risks and cultivating the friendship of
local agents so they would give more business to his company. On Saturday morning, sitting in the library, he would
put a check on each inspection slip as he finished glancing
over it, and when he had a pile of them he would hand
them to me and I would sit on the floor and arrange them
around me alphabetically, by towns, proud that I could be
of use to him. He left on Tuesday morning, carrying a grip
that was heavy with printed forms, and came home Friday
afternoon to a household that was seething with problems
he was not accustomed to dealing with. His sadness was of
the kind that is patient and without hope. He continued to
sleep in the bed he and my mother had shared, and tried to
act in a way she would have wanted him to, and I suspect
that as time passed he was less and less sure what that was.
He gave away her jewelry, and more important to me, her
clothes, so I could no longer open her closet door and
look at them.

I overheard one family friend after another assuring him
that there was no cure but time, and though he said, "Yes, I
know," I could tell he didn't believe them. Once a week he
would wind all the clocks in the house, beginning with the
grandfather's clock in the front hall. Their minute and hour
hands went round dependably and the light outside corrob-

orated what they said: it was breakfast time, it was late afternoon, it was night, with the darkness pressing against the windowpanes. What the family friends said is true. For some people. For others the hands of the clock can go round till kingdom come and not cure anything. I don't know by what means my father came to terms with his grief. All I know is that it was more than a year before the color came back into his face and he could smile when somebody said something funny.

When people spoke about my mother it was always in generalities—her wonderful qualities, her gift for making those around her happy, and so on—that didn't tell me anything I didn't know before. It was as if they couldn't see her clearly for what had happened to her. And to us. She didn't like having her picture taken and all we had was a few snapshots and one formal photograph, taken when she was in her early twenties, with her hair piled on top of her head and a black velvet ribbon around her throat. She was only thirty-eight when she died, but she had grown heavy, as women of that period tended to do. There was no question about the mouth or the soft brown eyes. The rest I did not recognize, though I was willing to believe that she had once looked like that. This picture didn't satisfy my father either, and he got the photographer who had taken it to touch it up so she would look more like a mature woman. The result was something I was quite sure my mother had never looked like—vague and idealized and as if she might not even remember who we were. My mother sometimes got excited and flew off the handle, but not this woman, who died before her time, leaving a grief-stricken husband and three motherless children. The retouched photograph came between me and the face I remembered, and it got harder and harder to recall my mother as she really was. After I couldn't remember any more except in a general way what she looked like, I could still remember the sound of her voice, and I clung to that. I also clung to the idea that if things remained exactly the way they were, if we were careful not to take a step in any direction from the place where we were now, we would somehow get back to the way it was before she died. I knew that this was not a rational belief, but the alternative—that when people die they are really gone and I would never see her again—was more than I could manage then or for a long time afterward.

When my father was an old man, he surprised me by re-marking that he understood what my mother's death meant to me but had no idea what to do about it. I think it would have been something if he had just said this. If he didn't, it was possibly because he thought there was nothing he or anybody else could do. Or he may have thought I would reject any help he tried to give me. As a small child I some-times had the earache, and I would go to him and ask him to blow cigar smoke in my ear. He would stop talking and draw me toward him and with his lips almost touching my ear breathe warm smoke into it. It was as good a remedy as any, and it was physically intimate. One night—I don't know how old I was, five or six, maybe—bedtime came and I kissed my mother good night as usual and then went over to my father and as I leaned toward him he said I was too old for that any more. By the standards of that time and that place I expect I was, but I had wanted to anyway. And how was I to express the feeling I had for him? He didn't say, then or ever. In that moment my feeling for him changed and became wary and unconfident.

All up and down Ninth Street there were children I could play with, and sometimes I did, but I preferred to play by myself. On the most beautiful spring day of the year I stayed in the house, reading *Tik-Tok of Oz*. And when I

grew tired of reading I shut myself up in a darkened room
and played with my postcard projector or with a toy theater
I had made out of shirt cardboards. All this worried my
father, both from the standpoint of my not being outdoors
enough and because if I continued to be interested in such
things, how on earth would I support myself when I grew
up? There was nothing comical or odd in his thinking this.
We are what we are, and he was a businessman, and in his
mind there was no better thing that one could be. From time
to time his hand came down on some elaborate fancy and I
had to pick up the pieces and go somewhere where he
wasn't in order to feel cheerful again. If he spoke impa-
tiently to me or with what seemed to me to be harshness, I
could not keep back the tears, which added to his annoyance.
As he turned away I had the feeling he had washed his hands
of me. Was I not the kind of little boy he wanted to have?
He didn't say that either. It is hard enough for adults to keep
their emotional reactions in something like balance. Children
simply feel what they feel, and I knew I was not the apple of
my father's eye.

   We were both creatures of the period. I doubt if the
heavy-businessman-father-and-the-oversensitive-artistic-son
syndrome exists any more. Fathers have become sympathetic and kiss their grown sons when they feel like it, and
who knows what oversensitive is, considering all there is to
be sensitive to.

When a sufficient number of months had been torn off the
calendar so that my mother's friends felt they could invite
my father to their dinner parties, they did. And he got
dressed up and went. They were matchmaking, of course,
and like all matchmakers had mixed motives. I doubt if he

needed their help. He was still only in his early forties, and he had always been handsome, and liked women, and it would have been strange if he hadn't found somebody who was willing to love him. I had no comprehension whatever of the sexual and emotional needs of a man of his age. He was simply my father, and I assumed that for the rest of his life he would be—"faithful to my mother's memory" is how I had heard grown people express it.

While he was having his social life, I was having mine. Our room at school decided to have a Halloween party and it was a question of where to have it. I offered our house and the offer was accepted. When I told my father he shook his head doubtfully and asked what I planned to do. I said I was going to carve a pumpkin and put some cornstalks around in the living room. He didn't think the party was at all a good idea, it would mean extra work for the house-keeper, and next time I'd better ask before I did something like that. Since I had committed myself, I could go ahead with it, provided it was confined to an empty maid's room and they used the back stairs. My mother wasn't there to tell him that this was unthinkable and so that's what happened. Deeply embarrassed, I led the teacher and my classmates through rooms that were brightly lit and had always been so hospitable, through the dining room to the pantry and up the narrow uninviting back stairs. Nobody seemed to find this in any way strange. I don't think it was much of a Halloween party. What has stayed in my mind all these years is a scene that occurred by the laundry basket in the back hall. The teacher had been chosen to be the "victim" and sat down on a chair and allowed herself to be blind-folded. At that point, ideas of propriety made me hesitate. I motioned to one of the girls, who took my place. When the teacher removed the blindfold she was smiling with pleasure because a young boy—because she *thought* a young boy had kissed her.

In telling me that he was going to be married my father was as gentle as he knew how to be. He didn't expect me to offer any objection, and wouldn't have been deflected from his purpose if I had.

A year or two before this, at the Country Club on a summer day, wandering idly near the caddie house I came upon a sight I didn't understand. I thought at first it was some new kind of animal. Then I retreated in horror. What I was looking at was a snake in the act of swallowing a frog that was too large and wouldn't go down. Neither would the idea that another woman was not only going to sit in my mother's place at the dinner table but also take her place in my father's heart.

Where a hardier boy would have run away from home or got in trouble with the police, I sat with my nose in a book so I wouldn't have to think about things I didn't like and couldn't prevent happening. It wasn't enough for me, or for my older brother and my younger brother and me, to slip through that door to the way things used to be, when the time came; my mother would expect us to bring my father with us. And if he was married to another woman, how could we?

We had moved from our fixed position and there was now no possibility of getting back to the way things were before she died. I could not tell whether the heavy feeling in my chest had to do with what might happen or with what had already happened and was irremediable.

The kindergarten run by Miss Lena Moose and Miss Lucy Sheffield was on the second floor of a building just off the courthouse square, and the young woman who became my stepmother used to go from house to house at nine o'clock in the morning, collecting the children. When we were all assembled, she walked us downtown. She must have been in her early twenties then. As a child she had lived on Ninth Street, though she didn't any more. At noon, on the day of my mother's funeral, when we went into the dining room she was there. I sat down at the table but I could not eat. My throat was blocked from crying. She came and stood behind my chair and talked to me, and urged me to eat some of the baked potato on my plate. For her sake, because she was young and pretty and because I had always liked her, I managed to do it. The taste of that baked potato has remained with me all the rest of my life.

In fairy tales the coming of a stepmother is never regarded as anything but a misfortune. Presumably this is not because of the great number of second wives who were unkind to the children of their husband's first marriage, though examples of this could be found, but because of the universal resentment on the children's part of an outsider. So that for the father to remarry is an act of betrayal not only of the dead mother but of them, no matter what the stepmother is like.

What strange and unlikely things are washed up on the shore of time. I have in my possession a tattered photograph album full of snapshots of my stepmother as a young woman. Very pretty and sweet she was, with a fur muff and a picture hat and her skirts almost to the floor. There are pictures of her with friends, with her mother and sister, with one or another of her four brothers, with elderly relatives on the front stoop of a turn-of-the-century house in, I think, Boston. There are two group pictures, taken by a local photographer, of a masquerade party—one with masks and one without, so that you can see who the pirate, the clown, the Columbine, etc., were. Half the people there I knew when I was growing up. And then more pictures of my step-mother: in Washington, D.C., during the First World War, with a thin-faced man in army uniform whom she was in love with at the time but did not marry; back in Lincoln, holding her sister's baby, and so on. What beautiful clothes. What glorious automobiles. What good times.

At the beginning and end of the album, pasted in what must have been blank places, since they run counter to the sequence, are a dozen pictures of my father. Except for the one where he is standing with a string of fish spread out on a rock beside him, he is always in a group of people. He has a golf stick in his hand. Or he is smoking a pipe. Or he is wearing a bathing suit and has one arm around my step-mother's waist and the other around a woman I don't recognize. And looking at these faded snapshots I see, the child that survives in me sees with a pang that—I am old enough to be that man's father, and he has been dead for nearly twenty years, and yet it troubles me that he was happy. Why? In some way his happiness was at that time (and for-ever after, it would seem) a threat to me. It was not the kind of happiness that children are included in, but why should that trouble me now? I do not even begin to under-stand it.

If I had by some supernatural sleight of hand managed to pull off that trick and brought my mother back from the cemetery and if we had continued to live the way we did before, we would have found ourselves on an island in a river of change, for it was the year 1921, and women had begun to cut off their hair and wear their skirts above their

knees and drink gin out of silver flasks in public. Now and
then one of them drank too much and had to be taken home.
The gossips had a great deal to shake their heads over. In
the light of what followed, the twenties seem on the whole
a charming, carefree period. So far as good manners are
concerned, it was the beginning of the end. When my
mother went riding with my father on Sunday morning
she rode sidesaddle (think of it!) and came out of the house
and down the steps of the front porch in a divided skirt that
swept the cement walk. I try to imagine her with bobbed
hair and her skirts above her knees and I fail utterly.

It was still possible to think, as my father did, that the
present was in every way an improvement over the past, and
that the future was bound to be even more satisfactory. He
also believed in keeping up with the times. When Prohibition
came in, he announced that he was ready to obey the Law
and give up drinking—by which he meant a glass of beer
or a shot of bourbon, in masculine company. When it turned
out that other people were not going to do this, he made his
own gin and bought rotgut whiskey from a bootlegger
named Coonhound Johnny, like his friends.

On one occasion he even overshot the mark. Friday afternoons I went to dancing school and pushed girls around in
the one-step, the fox trot, and the waltz. They held themselves at arm's length, their backs as stiff as a ramrod, their
manner remote. The dancing teacher was young and ani-
mated and something under five feet tall, which meant that
she was my height even though she wore very high heels.
There was also a class for adults on Thursday evenings, to
which my father and stepmother went before they were
married. One night they put their cheeks together and did a
new dance that they had been practising in private. It was
called the Toddle, and everybody stopped to look at

them, and the dancing teacher, very red in the face, asked them to leave the floor.

It is characteristic of my father that though he was angry at her and never went back, he did not remove me from the children's class. On Friday afternoon the dancing teacher kept me after the other boys and girls had gone. She was in trouble, though she didn't quite manage to say what it was. Did she sense that I was half on her side and nobody else much was? She had done the right thing, without stopping to think that the two people involved were of good family and she was a grass widow with two small children to support and from out of town. She may not, in fact, even have known who was and who wasn't of good family. I felt sorry for her, as I would have for anybody in tears. And disloyal to my father as I stood there listening to the things she said about him. And embarrassed that he was the object of scandal.

One of the things my mother loved about my father was that he was a natural musician. Hoping that this talent might have been inherited, she arranged for my older brother to take piano lessons from a nun who taught music in the Catholic school. When I was six I accompanied him to the house where the nuns lived, for my first music lesson. Sister Mary Anise showed me where to put my hands on the keyboard and I looked up at her teeth, which were frightfully crooked, and burst into tears. She told my brother to bring me back when I was seven—by which time she was wearing false teeth that were not crooked and I could look at her with equanimity. I was not musical and I didn't like to practise. What I did like was the lives of the composers, doled out to me one at a time in the form of unbound sheets of printed matter that had to be folded and sewed together at the spine, and a perforated sheet of illustrations to be pasted in at the appropriate places. In the first of these books I read how Johann Sebastian Bach's wicked elder brother was jealous of his talent and wouldn't let him have access to the music he wanted, so he got up in the night and copied it by moonlight, ruining his eyesight. I formed an attachment to the young put-upon Johann Sebastian Bach, and after him to Handel and his Water Music, and Haydn and Mozart and Beethoven and Schubert and Schumann and Mendelssohn and Wagner's operas and classical music in general. It didn't improve my playing. "Flat," my mother would call out from the next room, when I was practising at home. "E-flat, not E-natural." And I would get up from the piano stool and go look at the clock in the front hall.

My father kept a small victrola on top of the upright piano in the living room and after dinner, having played a new record through two or three times while he figured out the chords, he was off, he had it. He played ragtime and songs from the musicals of the period. He had a beautiful touch and people loved to hear him. One day he sat down at the piano with me and tried to teach me how to play by ear. I didn't understand one word he was saying.

It gave him no pleasure to hear me stumble through "The Shepherd Boy's Prayer," and also he wanted me to like his kind of music, so, when I was twelve, without inquiring how I felt about it, he took me away from Sister Mary Anise and Bach and Handel and Haydn, and arranged for me to take lessons from a young married woman who played the organ in the Catholic church and was my stepmother's closest friend. The piece she gave me to learn, at my father's suggestion, was "Alice Blue Gown." I liked her but I came to have a deep dislike for that inane song as, week after week, I played it and nothing else. I also made no progress. I had

found a small plot of ground on which I could oppose my
father without being actively disobedient.

Because he was finishing out a period of mourning, which in
those days had to be three years, roughly, or there was talk,
he and my stepmother waited. She was in California for a
while and when I went for my music lesson I would be given
a fat envelope that had come in the mail inside another envelope addressed to my music teacher. Nobody explained
that this was so the housekeeper couldn't steam the envelope
open and read what was inside; instead, they acted as though
it was the most natural thing in the world for a twelve-year-
old boy to be bringing a love letter home to his father.

The reason life is so strange is that so often people have no
choice, but in this case I think convenience entered into it: I
mean, my father could have rented a box at the post office.
He may have been deterred by the fact that if he was seen
entering and leaving the post office and taking mail out of a
box, people would very soon have guessed why. So in short
he had no choice either, about that or about selling the house,
which was so full of associations with my mother. In a matter of two or three weeks after he put it on the market, it
was bought by a man who had had enough of farming and
wanted to live in town. One day while I was in school the
moving men came and what furniture my father hadn't
managed to sell or give away ended up in a much smaller
house that he had rented on an unpaved street out near the
edge of town.

I went straight home from school to the new house.
Though as a grown man I have often stood and looked at the
old house, I have never been inside it since that day, when a
great many objects that I remember and would like to be
reunited with disappeared without a trace: Victorian wal-

nut sofas and chairs that my fingers had absently traced every knob and scroll of, mahogany tables, worn Oriental rugs, gilt mirrors, pictures, big square books full of photographs that I knew by heart. If they hadn't disappeared then, they would have on some other occasion, life being, as Ortega y Gasset somewhere remarks, in itself and forever shipwreck.

The rented house had no yard to speak of, the porch steps were ten feet from the front sidewalk, and our house and the house next door were identical. The bites that woke me in the night proved to be bedbugs, concealed under a loose corner of the wallpaper, and the exterminator took care of them. My father probably thought that since we were not going to stay there it didn't matter too much what the house was like. Or there may not, at that moment, have been anything better. I used to stand and compare the two identical houses, detail by detail, the way you compare repeats in wallpaper hoping to find some small difference. I did not so much miss the old house as blot it completely out of my mind. We had gone down in the world and there didn't seem to be anything to do but make the best of it. Ninth Street had the air of having been there since the beginning of time. Generations of children had grown up there, leaving their bicycles where people could fall over them, making leaf houses, climbing trees, playing run-sheep-run on summer evenings. The unpaved street we were now living on had no past and no future but only a wan present in which it was hard to think of anything to do.

One evening in October my father and Grace McGrath came down the stairs in her sister's house and were married on the landing, by the Catholic priest, who couldn't marry them in a church because my father was a Protestant. I was the only person present under the age of thirty. My older brother was away at college, my younger brother

asleep in his crib. Now was the moment to forget about that
door I had walked through without thinking, and about the
void that could sometimes be bridged in dreams, and about
the way things used to be when my mother was alive. Instead,
I clung to them more tightly than ever, even as I was being
drawn willy-nilly into my father's new life.

3

The New House

The small towns in central Illinois nearly all owe their existence to the coming of the railroads in the decade before the Civil War. I have always had the impression that Lincoln is in some way different from the others but perhaps that is only because I lived there. It is the county seat and has two coal mines, now worked out. It has never had any sizable factories, and owes its modest prosperity to the surrounding farmland. In the year 1921 the shade trees that everywhere lined the residential streets had had time to come full size and made the town seem older than it actually was. It was not easy to tell when the houses were built, because their age was so frequently disguised by subsequent additions, and so they seemed timeless and as inseparably a part of the people who lived in them as their voices or their names or the way they combed their hair.

My father found most old things oppressive, but especially old houses with high ceilings and odd-shaped rooms that opened one out of another, offering a pleasant vista that required a great deal of coal to heat in the harsh Illinois winters. Intending to escape all this by building, he bought a double lot in Park Place, a subdivision so recently laid out that the trees were only five feet tall and had to be staked against the north wind. All but two of the existing houses were on the right-hand side of the street, facing a cow pasture that I think has not been built on to this day. The building lots were narrow and the houses much closer together than they were in the old part of town, but there was an ornamental brick gateway leading into the street and a grass plot down the center, and it was fashionable. In present-day Lincoln it is fashionable to live clear out in the country, surrounded by cornfields.

My father and my stepmother had seen a stucco house in Bloomington that they liked, and they got an architect to copy the exterior and then the three of them fiddled with the interior plans until they were satisfactory. I was shown on the blueprints where my room was going to be. In a short time the cement foundation was poured and the framing was up and you could see the actual size and shape of the rooms. I used to go there after school and watch the carpenters hammering: *pung, pung, pung, kapung, kapung, kapung, kapung.* . . . They may have guessed that I was waiting for them to pick up their tools and go home so I could climb around on the scaffolding but they didn't tell me I couldn't do this, or in fact pay any attention to me at all. And I had the agreeable feeling, as I went from one room to the next by walking through the wall instead of a doorway, or looked up and saw blue sky through the rafters, that I had found a way to get around the way things were.

When, wandering through the Museum of Modern Art, I come upon the piece of sculpture by Alberto Giacometti with the title "Palace at 4 A.M.," I always stand and look at it—partly because it reminds me of my father's new house in its unfinished state and partly because it is so beautiful. It is about thirty inches high and sufficiently well known that I probably don't need to describe it. But anyway, it is made of wood, and there are no solid walls, only thin uprights and horizontal beams. There is the suggestion of a

classic pediment and of a tower. Flying around in a room
at the top of the palace there is a queer-looking creature
with the head of a monkey wrench. A bird? a cross between
a male ballet dancer and a pterodactyl? Below it, in a kind
of freestanding closet, the backbone of some animal. To the
left, backed by three off-white parallelograms, what could
be an imposing female figure or one of the more important
pieces of a chess set. And, in about the position a basketball
ring would occupy, a vertical, hollowed-out spatulate shape
with a ball in front of it.

It is all terribly spare and strange, but no stranger than
the artist's account of how it came into being: "This object
took shape little by little in the late summer of 1932; it re-
vealed itself to me slowly, the various parts taking their exact
form and their precise place within the whole. By autumn
it had attained such reality that its actual execution in space
took no more than one day. It is related without any doubt
to a period in my life that had come to an end a year before,
when for six whole months hour after hour was passed in
the company of a woman who, concentrating all life in
herself, magically transformed my every moment. We used
to construct a fantastic palace at night—days and nights had
the same color, as if everything happened just before daybreak; throughout the whole time I never saw the sun—a
very fragile palace of matchsticks. At the slightest false
move a whole section of this tiny construction would col-
lapse. We would always begin it over again. I don't know
why it came to be inhabited by a spinal column in a cage—
the spinal column this woman sold me one of the very first
nights I met her on the street—and by one of the skeleton
birds that she saw the very night before the morning in
which our life together collapsed—the skeleton birds that
flutter with cries of joy at four o'clock in the morning very
high above the pool of clear, green water where the ex-

tremely fine, white skeletons of fish float in the great un-roofed hall. In the middle there rises the scaffolding of a tower, perhaps unfinished or, since its top has collapsed, per-haps also broken. On the other side there appeared the statue of a woman, in which I recognize my mother, just as she ap-pears in my earliest memories. The mystery of her long black dress touching the floor troubled me; it seemed to me like a part of her body, and aroused in me a feeling of fear and confusion. . . ."

I seem to remember that I went to the new house one win-ter day and saw snow descending through the attic to the upstairs bedrooms. It could also be that I never did any such thing, for I am fairly certain that in a snapshot album I have lost track of there was a picture of the house taken in the circumstances I have just described, and it is possible that I am remembering that rather than an actual experience. What we, or at any rate what I, refer to confidently as memory—meaning a moment, a scene, a fact that has been subjected to a fixative and thereby rescued from oblivion—is really a form of storytelling that goes on continually in the mind and often changes with the telling. Too many conflicting emotional interests are involved for life ever to be wholly acceptable, and possibly it is the work of the storyteller to rearrange things so that they conform to this end. In any case, in talk-ing about the past we lie with every breath we draw.

Before the stairway was in, there was a gaping hole in the center of the house and you had to use the carpenters' rickety ladder to get to the second floor. One day I looked down through this hole and saw Cletus Smith standing on a pile of lumber looking at me. I suppose I said, "Come on up." Anyway, he did. We stood looking out at the unlit streetlamp, through a square opening that was some day go-ing to be a window, and then we climbed up another lad-der and walked along horizontal two-by-sixes with our arms outstretched, teetering like circus acrobats on the high wire. We could have fallen all the way through to the basement and broken an arm or a leg but we didn't.

Boys don't need much of an excuse to get on well together, if they get on at all. I was glad for his company, and pleased when he turned up the next day. If I saw him now the way he was then, I don't know that I would recognize him. I seem to remember his smile, and that he had large hands and feet for a boy of thirteen. And Cletus Smith isn't his real name.

Did I know him because he was in my room at school? I try to picture him standing at the blackboard and can't. It is so long ago. Were we in the same Boy Scout troop, which would have meant that at some time during that fall we had studied the Scout manual together and practised tying reef knots and clove hitches and running bowlines, and considered what merit badges we would try for next? I don't know the answer. I only know that I knew him. From somewhere. And that we played together in that unfinished house day after day, risking our necks and breathing in the rancid odor of sawdust and shavings and fresh-cut lumber.

Ninth Street was an extension of home, and perfectly safe. Nobody ever picked on me there. When I passed beyond Ninth Street, it could be rough going. The boys in the eighth grade dominated the school yard before school and at recess time. They were, by turns, good-natured in a patronizing way, or mean, or foulmouthed about girls, or single-mindedly bent on improving their proficiency in some sport. Sometimes they would go to the trouble of twisting a younger boy's arm behind his back or put a foot out and trip him as he ran past, and if he fell and hurt himself they were happy for a whole quarter of an hour afterward, but their attention seldom settled on any one boy for very long.

Looking back, it seems clear enough that I brought my

difficulties on myself. To begin with, I was as thin as a stick. In any kind of competitive game, my mind froze and I became half paralyzed. The baseball could be counted on to slip through my overanxious fingers. Nobody wanted me on their team. I was a character. I also had the unfortunate habit, when called on in class, of coming up with the right answer. It won me a smile of approval from the teacher, and it was nice to see my name on the Honor Roll. It was not nice to be chased home from school by two coal miners' sons who were in the same room with me but only because they could not escape from the truant officer. Nowhere was I safe against them—neither in the classroom, where their eyes were always on me, or in the school yard, where they danced around me, pushing me off balance and trying to get me to fight back so they could clean up on me.

All this took place in plain sight of everybody, all the boys I had grown up with, and no hand was ever raised in my defense, nobody ever came to my rescue—I expect partly because they had their own vulnerabilities and did not want to be singled out for attack, but obviously there was something about me that invited it. Since I did not know what it was, I couldn't do anything to change it, and any emotion I felt—physical inadequacy, fear, humiliation, the whole repertoire of the adolescent—showed in my face. I was such easy game that I wonder that their pleasure in tormenting me lasted as long as it did. When they were fourteen they dropped out of school and I never saw them again. Where else could they have gone but down in the mine with their fathers? If somebody told me they had contracted black lung I don't know that I could manage to be sorry.

The gap between my older brother and me was too great for me to emulate his pleasures or contribute to them, and I would have been glad for a brother nearer my own age, to defend me when I got in trouble, and to do things with.

At about this time, one of my mother's friends, a woman I knew but not very well, invited me to come to her house after school on Friday and stay until Sunday afternoon. She had a son who was a year or two older than I was and everything a boy that age ought to be—open and easy with adults, bright in school, and beyond being pushed around by his contemporaries. I slept in the same room with him and I was with him all day Saturday and Sunday. Without any experience to go on, I tried to be a good guest. Most of the time he was friendly, and then suddenly he would mutter something under his breath that I could not quite hear and that I knew from a heaviness in my heart was the word "sissy." I ignored it, not knowing what else to do; not having enough experience of the world to take my toothbrush and pyjamas and go home, leaving him to explain to his mother why I wasn't there. At bedtime, standing by the wide-open window of his room, he had me do setting-up exercises with him. He was patient when I didn't do them right, and also funny, and it was so nice to be doing something with another boy for a change. But then he muttered that word under his breath that I wasn't supposed to be able to say that he had actually said. He was exactly the kind of boy I would have liked to be, and I was ready to imitate him in any way I could. One minute I was encouraged to do this and the next I felt—I was made to feel—that he despised me. Probably all it amounted to was that his mother had decided on this act of kindness without consulting him, and he was angry because my being there had spoiled his Saturday. In any case, the point I am trying to make is that it was a new experience for me to have the companionship of another boy day after day. Whatever I suggested doing we did. I never asked Cletus if there wasn't something he'd rather be doing, because he was always ready to do what I wanted to do. It occurs to me now that he was not very different from an imaginary playmate. When I was with him, if I said something the boys in the school yard would have jeered at, he let the opportunity pass and went on carefully teetering with one foot in front of the other, or at most, without glancing in my direction, which would have endangered his balance, nodded.

I supposed he must have liked me somewhat or he wouldn't have been there. And that he was glad for my companionship. He didn't act as if there was some other boy waiting for him to turn up. He must have understood that I was going to live in this house when it was finished, but it didn't occur to me to wonder where he lived.

When I was a child I told my mother everything. After she died I learned that it was better to keep some things to myself. My father represented authority, which meant—to me —that he could not also represent understanding. And because there was an element of cruelty in my older brother's teasing (as, of course, there is in all teasing) I didn't trust him, though I perfectly well could have, about larger matters. Anyway, I didn't tell Cletus about my shipwreck, as we sat looking down on the whole neighborhood, and he didn't tell me about his. When the look of the sky informed us that it was getting along toward suppertime, we climbed down and said "So long" and "See you tomorrow," and went our separate ways in the dusk. And one evening this casual parting turned out to be for the last time. We were separated by that pistol shot.

There was never any real doubt about who had killed Lloyd Wilson. The only person who had any reason to do it was Clarence Smith, Cletus's father. Among the things that Cletus failed to tell me was the fact that he had grown up in the country. He had only been living in town a few months. His mother had sued his father for a divorce, the grounds

being extreme and repeated cruelty. His father then filed a
cross bill charging her with infidelity and naming Lloyd
Wilson, who lived on the adjoining farm, as corespondent.

The Lincoln *Courier-Herald* was, and is, a self-respecting
small-town newspaper and it did not feel called upon to
provide the salacious details, which are safely buried in the
court records. I think it highly unlikely that Cletus was
present at the divorce trial. How much did he know?
Enough, probably. Enough so that it was preferable to play
with a boy he hardly knew than with somebody he might be
tempted to confide in—if there was any such person.

When the divorce proceedings went against him, Cletus's
father sold his lease and gave up farming and moved in with
Cletus's grandparents in town. He was depressed and given
to fits of weeping. And he could not keep from talking
about his troubles. Men who had known him for many years
took to crossing over to the other side of the street when
they saw him coming.

Lloyd Wilson confessed to his two brothers that he lived
in fear of an attack on his life, and they told him he ought
to leave town immediately. Like a figure in a dream, he took
all the steps he should have taken, but in slow motion. He
went to see the woman whose land he farmed and asked to
be released from his contract, which did not expire until
March. He consulted a lawyer.

On the morning that he was killed he left the barn door
open wide so as to catch the morning light when it came.
The light from his lantern must have fallen just short of the
toe of the murderer's boot.

I assume that I knew all this once, since it was published in
the evening paper and I was old enough to read. In the course
of time the details of the murder passed from my mind,

and what I thought happened was so different from what actually did happen that it might almost have been something I made up out of whole cloth. And I might have gone right on thinking that Cletus's father had come home unexpectedly and found Cletus's mother in bed with a man and killed them both, but one day, as if I had suddenly broken through a brick wall, I realized that there are always sources of information about the past other than one's own recollection, and that I didn't need to remain in total ignorance about something that interested me so deeply. I wrote to my stepcousin Tom Perry and asked him if he could dig up for me those issues of the *Courier-Herald* that had anything in them about the murder of Lloyd Wilson. He reported back to me that the *Courier*'s file (the *Herald* was dropped a long time ago) did not go back to the year 1922 and that the public library had destroyed its file six months before and what I'd better do was apply to the Illinois State Historical Society in Springfield. It was as if I was inquiring into the funeral of Abraham Lincoln. But anyway, I did as he said, and the Historical Society sent me, from its microfilm library, photostatic copies, not always entirely legible, of eight issues of a newspaper once as familiar to me as the back of my hand. It was, of course, much more than I had asked for, a small segment of the past, remote and yet in perfect focus, like something seen through the wrong end of a pair of binoculars: ads for movies starring Norma Talmadge and Wallace Reid, good quality of men's suits at Griesheim's clothing store at $7, and many other things equally hard to believe.

I don't know where the office and printing plant of the Lincoln *Courier* is now; only that it isn't where it used to be, on North Kickapoo Street, half a block from the courthouse square.

Several of the pieces about the murder were written by

the editor, whom I remember as a high-strung, dark-haired
man with a green eyeshade and a cigarette in the corner of
his mouth. His stories give the impression of being dashed
off in the last minutes before the paper went to press; that is
to say, they are repetitious and disordered and full of not
very acute speculation. Also of clichés and reticences which
the ideas of the period no doubt required. People are quoted
as saying things I have trouble believing that they actually
said, at least in those words. I am reasonably sure, for example, that Cletus's father did not say to a man he met on
the street the day before the murder, "I am broken and a
failure and I have nothing for which to live." Nobody I
know in the Middle West has ever gone out of his way to
avoid ending a sentence with a preposition. But it isn't fair,
in any case, to blame that overworked small-town newspaper
editor for not writing as well as Roughead. Especially since
I am indebted to him for any knowledge I have of what
happened.

The sheriff was on the point of taking some prisoners to
the courthouse for trial when the undertaker called him.
The deputy sheriff and the coroner went out to the Wilson
farm and Fred Wilson showed them the stall Lloyd Wilson
was in, the pail that had only a little milk in it, the milking
stool, the gloves that he always wore when he was milking
and that were still on his hands when they found him. Near
the door of the cow barn the two men from town saw some
footprints, which they covered with boards so they would
stay fresh. All morning, search parties beat over the muddy
fields and along the banks of a creek that ran through both
farms. The bloodhounds arrived from Springfield, by train,
and were taken to the scene of the crime. Two hundred
people were there waiting for them. The footprints were un-
covered and the dogs were led to the cow barn and un-
leashed. Sniffing, they circled an implement shed and a hay-

stack and returned to the barn and then they jumped a barbed-wire fence and took off, with a pack of excited men running after them. Just before the dogs got to the farmhouse Clarence Smith had recently moved out of, they turned aside, at a gate, and followed the lane out to the public road. After pausing at the mailbox they crossed over to the other side of the road and lost the scent. Twice they were led back to the cow barn and let loose. The first time, they went into the yard of the Smith farm and up onto the porch. The second time, they turned aside again, into a cornfield, and followed a trail of footprints until they ended up on the hard road, a quarter of a mile west of the lane.

Clarence Smith had sold his lease to a younger man named James Walker. After the bloodhounds were taken back to town, Walker came out of the farmhouse and walked out to the public road. A handful of men lingered by the entrance to the lane and, moved by a floating curiosity, they gathered around him while he pulled down the flap of the mailbox. What were they expecting? At most a letter or two that they would not be allowed to read and yesterday's *Courier-Herald*. In the mailbox was an object so startling that they all stepped back and waited. James Walker took the gold watch out of the mailbox and opened the case and found the initials "C.S." It could only be Clarence Smith's watch, but when was it left there and for what reason? James Walker drove in to town and turned it over to the sheriff, who considered the possibility that it was a plant, put there by someone other than Clarence Smith to make it appear that he was the murderer.

That evening, the sheriff went to the house of Clarence Smith's parents and learned that they had no idea where their son was. Neither had anyone else. He was last seen leaving the Grand Theater at 10:45 on the night before Lloyd Wilson was killed. The State's attorney didn't issue a warrant charging Cletus's father with the murder. He was merely wanted for questioning. The description sent to the police throughout the state reads: "Age 40 years, height 5 feet 7 inches, weight 165 pounds, light brown hair slightly bald."

Neighbors reported that they had seen a strange automobile waiting near the Wilson farm on the night before the murder. One of them said that the automobile waited in the lane just off the hard road for at least two hours. He saw it for the last time at about nine o'clock, just before he went to bed. Another neighbor said that the automobile was not in the lane but at the edge of the hard road, and that it was standing with the lights turned off. Since Clarence Smith did not own a car, this raised the question of whether he might have had an accomplice.

There was a rumor that he was seen boarding the trolley car that ran between Peoria, Lincoln, and Springfield, on the day of the murder. Also that he had registered at a hotel in Springfield and that same night had received a long-distance telephone call there. Given the chance to believe something so interesting, people did, though the hotel denied that he had been there, and the person who saw him board the trolley never came forward. The rumor that he had a large sum of money on his person when he disappeared couldn't have been true either, since the money from the sale of his lease could all be accounted for.

There was another angle to the case that the *Courier* felt obliged to consider. In the spring of the year before he was killed, Lloyd Wilson's wife left him, taking their four girls, the youngest of whom was a baby eleven months old, and moved to town. She did not divorce him but got a legal separation. By the terms of this agreement he had to pay her

$9,000, which in 1921 was a lot of money. My father's new house only cost $12,000, including the land it was built on. The settlement Lloyd Wilson made on his wife may have represented all the money he had.

I don't know what she looked like. Most farm women of her age were reduced by hard work and frequent child-bearing to a common denominator of plainness. I fancy, as people used to say when I was a child—I fancy that this was true of Lloyd Wilson's wife and that it was not true of Cletus's mother, but there is no warrant for my thinking this, and the simple truth is that though so much is made of the woman's beauty in love stories, passion does not require it. Plato's idea that lovers were originally one person, the two parts having become separated and desiring to be joined, is as good an explanation as any for what cannot in the mind of an outsider ever be convincingly accounted for.

The names and ages of the Wilson children were printed in the paper. Probably through happenstance, the names and ages of Clarence Smith's were not.

Cletus's mother had been an orphan and was brought up by an aunt and uncle, who lived in town. When she left Cletus's father she moved back to the house she grew up in. The *Courier-Herald* gives the address, and I asked my cousin to see if there was a house at that address now. He reported back that there was and that it was one of a row of frame houses opposite the fairgrounds. Somewhat down at the heels, he said, and painted white, and like a lot of other small houses in town.

What the newspaper refers to as "the estrangement" oc-curred during the summer after Wilson's wife left him. "A year ago," the *Courier-Herald* goes on to say, "there were no better friends than Wilson and Smith. They were often in town together. If Smith bought a cigar for himself he also bought one for Wilson, who did the same. In an argument they stuck up for each other against all comers, and people often spoke about what bosom friends they were. Smith is considered, by people who knew him, to be a quiet, reserved man."

The only photograph I have ever seen of him, or of Lloyd Wilson, was printed on the front page of the *Courier-Herald*. Since it is a photostatic copy, black and white—or rather, brown and white—are reversed. Even so, they look enough alike to be taken for brothers. No doubt Cain and Abel loved each other, in their way, quite as much as, or even more than, David and Jonathan.

There are many questions I did not find the answer to by reading those old newspapers. For example, from whom did Cletus's mother learn about the murder? And how soon? And what happened then—hysterics, in front of her two sons? And what about the six-year-old child who was sent to the barn to see what was keeping his father so long? Were he and his brother peering out through a lace curtain when the bloodhounds went baying across the fields in pursuit of the man who had killed their father? Or did the housekeeper draw them away from the window? She was a countrywoman, and you don't see such sights every day. Chances are that all three of them were peering out of the window, unless the little boys' mother had already come for them.

For several days new details kept turning up: "It is said on high authority that Wilson and Mrs. Smith corresponded frequently since the Smith divorce last fall, and during the time that Smith was paying alimony to his former wife. It is believed that Smith knew of this alleged fact and brooded over the situation. Mrs. Smith is said to have been afraid of her former husband, and this fear is believed to have been communicated to Wilson. . . . Sheriff Ahrens called in a former farm hand of Smith's who had testified for him during the trial. This man had been working in the Coonsburg vicinity, had been regularly employed there, and had not seen Smith since a week ago Saturday night when he came out of the bathroom of the local barber shop and saw Smith waiting for a shave." And so on.

James Walker told the reporter from the *Courier-Herald* that one day shortly after Clarence Smith left the farm and he took possession, he came out of the woodshed and saw Smith standing on the porch. Walker said he was all by himself at the time, and glad to have somebody to talk to. When Smith said, "Do you mind if I have a look around?" he said, "Go ahead, help yourself"—as anybody would under the circumstances. But when Smith came back again a few days later and spent a long time in the barn and then went into one shed after another, Walker grew uneasy. If Smith had lost something why didn't he say what it was? It turned out that Walker himself had lost something instead, a small anvil. He was positive he had brought it with him when he moved, and so far as he knew there was no way Clarence Smith could have carried it off with him, but neither could the anvil have walked off by itself.

James Walker wrote to his wife and asked her to join him immediately, and after that Clarence Smith didn't come any more.

The day after Walker found the watch he found Clarence Smith's overcoat, in a storm buggy. The deputy sheriff, searching the barns and outbuildings with a flashlight, had seen it and thought it belonged to the new tenant. Kept warm by the coat and some lap robes, Clarence Smith had spent the night before the murder on his own farm and in the morning concealed himself behind a haystack and waited for Lloyd Wilson's lantern to come bobbing across the pasture.

Cletus's grandfather, when he was interviewed by that same reporter, said that if his son had committed the murder while mentally unbalanced from jealousy he wouldn't be found alive; he wouldn't want to live.

Cletus's mother, perhaps too distraught to be charitable, said, "I do not believe he killed himself. I think he carried out plans for his escape." What plans? There is no evidence that he had made any.

Partly out of fear and partly to get away from curiosity-seekers, Walker and his wife moved into temporary quarters in town. The sheriff's office was kept busy answering calls from people who wanted to know if Clarence Smith had been found. Most of them had heard that he had drowned himself in the gravel pit. The *Courier-Herald* was at some pains to scotch this rumor also: "Deputy William Duffy, who conducted a thorough examination of the gravel pit the morning of the murder, does not believe that Smith or any other person drowned himself in the pit. The earth around it was soft, due to the thaw. On two sides the bank was steep and tracks would have shown clearly. At the point where it would have been possible to dive from a springboard, the water was shallow and a person would have had to wade out in the shallows before reaching deep water. Encircling the entire pit, looking for tracks in the soft earth, Mr. Duffy found absolutely nothing."

On Friday, the third of February, fifteen days after Lloyd Wilson's body was found leaning against a partition in his barn, another body was fished up from the bottom of Deer Creek gravel pit, where the deputy sheriff said it couldn't be. It was lying face down across the dredging bucket. Cletus's father, not wanting to live, had shot himself through the head. Dangling from his right wrist, at the end of a shoe-

string, was a .38 revolver with two empty chambers. A flashlight protruded from his coat pocket. A strand of baling
wire was wound around his neck and waist. Until it was
severed by the dredging bucket it had attached the body to
whatever the heavy weight was that was holding it down.
In going through the other pockets the undertaker found a
razor still deeply stained with red, a bloody handkerchief,
a watch chain, and several shotgun shells.

At the coroner's inquest, the only witnesses were the
sheriff and the three men who worked at the gravel pit. The
jury returned the following verdict: "We, the undersigned
jurors, do find that Clarence C. Smith came to his death by
a gunshot wound inflicted by his own hand, with suicidal
intent." There was no effort to establish a motive for the
suicide and no mention of the murder of Lloyd Wilson. At
the final hearing in the murder case, the verdict was "Death
from a gunshot wound inflicted by an unknown hand."

Several hundred people tried to get a look at Clarence
Smith's body while it was at the undertaker's and were
turned away. The funeral was in his father's house. "Rever-
end A. S. Hubbard, pastor of the First Baptist Church, was
in charge of the services. A male quartet, standing on the
stair landing, gave a number of selections. Pallbearers were
Joseph McElhiney, John Holmes, Frank Mitchell, and Roy
Anderson. Numerous floral tokens of sympathy were received by the family and the funeral was one of the largest
held in Lincoln in some time."

Cletus's father was not buried at the crossroads with a
stake through his heart but in the cemetery along with everybody else. The day after the funeral a gunstock was
found floating on the surface of the gravel pit. The following afternoon the dredging bucket brought up the rest of
the gun. In the barrel was a defective shell. When the shotgun failed to go off, the shell jammed, and the ejector didn't

remove it. And so Lloyd Wilson was killed with a revolver instead.

Cletus's grandfather was summoned to the sheriff's office to identify the gun and said he knew his son had a shotgun but he didn't know what it looked like or remember having seen the gun among the things his son brought with him when he moved from the farm. The sheriff then asked if Clarence Smith's sons hunted with him. "Identification of the gun"—I am quoting from the *Courier-Herald*—"was made this afternoon by the oldest son of Clarence C. Smith, who recognized the manufacturer's mark. The boy has a bicycle of the same make." Between the time that Cletus and I climbed down from the scaffolding and went our separate ways and the moment when he was confronted with the broken gun in the sheriff's office, he must have crossed over the line into maturity, and though he is referred to as a boy, wasn't one any longer.

Shortly after this his mother wrote to Lloyd Wilson's housekeeper asking that a photograph she had given him be returned to her. The *Courier-Herald* got hold of this letter and published one sentence from it: "I am the most miserable woman in the world."

4

In the School Corridor

I have a hazy half-recollection, which I do not trust, of sitting and staring at Cletus's empty desk at school. Somebody—I think it was my grandmother—said his grandmother came and took him away. It cannot have been true; he had only one grandmother and she was living right there in town. What probably happened is that his mother kept him out of school, and when she left Lincoln he went with her.

I didn't wonder what the evening paper meant precisely when it said that Cletus's father had accused his mother of having been intimate with the murdered man. I wouldn't at that age have been so innocent as to think it meant they were on friendly terms with each other. When I thought about the matter at all I thought about the ear, which was never found. I knew it was a most terrible thing that had happened to Cletus and that he would forever be singled out by it, but I didn't try to put myself in his place or even think that maybe I ought to find out where he lived and get on my bicycle and go see him. It was as if his father had shot and killed him too.

The carpenters and plumbers and electricians finally stopped getting in each other's way and left the new house entirely to the painters. I came home with white paint on my clothes and my father suggested that I stay away from Park

Place until the paint on the woodwork was dry. He was exasperated at the architect and at himself; if the concrete foundation had been sunk two or three feet lower into the ground, it wouldn't have required a great many loads of expensive topsoil to bring the lawn up to the necessary level. The day we moved in, Grace, overtired, dropped a bottle of iodine she was putting in the medicine cabinet of the upstairs bathroom and it fell into the washstand and broke. She and I spent our first evening in the new house scrubbing at what looked like bloodstains on the shining white wall.

The house was too new to be comfortable. It was like having to spend a lot of time with a person you didn't know very well. And I missed the way it used to be when there was no roof yet and the underflooring was littered with shavings and bent nails and pieces of wood I could almost but not quite think what to do with. Now there was nothing on the floor but rugs and you couldn't do daring things because if you did you might leave a mark on the wallpaper.

My father was always away during the middle of the week, my little brother spent two or three days at a time with my grandmother, who idolized him, and so Grace and I were often alone together. The people who lived in the houses all up and down the street were either related to her or her close friends. They were in and out of one another's houses all day long, and several afternoons a week they sat down to bridge tables. Expertly shuffling and reshuffling cards, they went to work. Auction, this was. Contract bridge hadn't yet supplanted it. Once, looking over Grace's shoulder, I saw her make a grand slam in clubs when the highest trump card in her hand was the nine. The women serenely doubled and redoubled each other's bids without ever losing their way in the intricacies of some piece of gossip, and the one who was adding up the score was still able to deplore, with the others, the shockingness of some new

novel that they had all put their names down for at the
library.

Fourteen was when boys graduated into long trousers and
since I hadn't yet arrived at that age I was still wearing corduroy knickerbockers. When I couldn't stop reading *A Tale
of Two Cities*, I put my long black cotton stockings across
the bottom of the bedroom door so my father wouldn't see
the crack of light and come in and tell me to go to sleep.
I had a one-tube radio set in my room, on the desk where I
studied. Above it, on the wall, was a map of North America,
with colored pins for all the radio stations I had picked up.
The pin that gave me the most pleasure was stuck at Havana,
Cuba, which I got only once. My ears hurt from the head-
phones and my feet were cold all winter long. My room
was on the northwest corner of the house and the hot-air
registers didn't do what was expected of them. And once
something happened that was so strange I couldn't get over
it. I heard Eggy Rinehart, two blocks away, call his mother
to the telephone. The radio set had picked up his voice out
of the air, but *how?* From the telephone wires? Nobody
could tell me.

When I came home from Scout meeting, the aerial on the
roof showed faintly against the stars. Before I walked into
the house I left the front walk and went and peered through
the crack of light between the drawn shade and the sill of
the living-room window. I wanted to make sure that my
father and Grace weren't having a "party." The word
had undergone a sinister metamorphosis. Originally it meant
ice cream in molds and other children arriving with presents
for me, or if it was a grown-up party then the best linen
tablecloth and place cards and little paper cups full of nuts
and a centerpiece of cut flowers from the greenhouse. And
more spoons and forks than usual. During Prohibition it
came to mean people getting together for the purpose of

drinking. Gossip made it sound worse than it was; there were limits. But I didn't know what they were and therefore assumed that there weren't any, and that if "parties" were not orgies exactly they were in that general area. Among Grace's friends were a handsome raven-haired woman who had a year or two before lost her husband and a humorous unmarried woman who worked at the bank. They were both at our house a good deal and my father referred to them jocosely as his harem. I knew that they weren't really, but what was I to think when I heard them laughing about how Lois went upstairs and took off all her clothes (at my mother's parties people didn't do such things) and came down wrapped in a bath towel and did the hootchie-kootchie dance? Anyway, I didn't want to blunder into something like that, so I looked before I walked into the house.

After a short while, all this I now think rather jolly behavior had stopped. It was merely a manifestation of the times and did not reflect their true personalities. They settled down into something like the ordinary quiet life of most married couples.

Grace could whistle like nobody's business, and I have a vivid memory of her rendition of "Here's to the heart that beats for me, true as the stars above. / Here's to the day when mine she'll be. Here's to the girl I love," as she made her way backwards down the stairs with a dust mop. It is like a still from an old movie. She never gets to the bottom of the stairs. In the remaining ten years before I took off for good, she was never impatient with me and I don't think I was ever rude to her. There was enough self-control in that household for six families. Unlike the wicked stepmother in the fairy tales, she had a gentle nature and could not bear any kind of altercation. And it was not in her to wrestle, like Jacob with the angel, until I stopped being faithful to a dead woman and accepted her as my mother. Instead she chose the role of the go-between. When my older brother had a Saturday-night date and wanted my father to let him have the car, he enlisted her aid and went off with the car keys in his pocket.

Grace's mother lived directly across the street from us with her son Ted, who was at that time a bachelor. Mrs. McGrath was a stately, warm-hearted old woman, much looked up to by her children. Grace's brothers were jovial, exceedingly kind men who, together, on next to nothing, had started a sand and gravel business and been successful. They loved to tell funny stories and whenever they were gathered together there was the sound of laughter. They also confused me by treating me as if I were a genuine relation. I didn't so much hold out against them as proceed with caution.

In that insufficiently heated bedroom on the northwest corner of the house in Park Place I was taken by surprise by the first intimations of a pleasure that I did not at first know how to elicit from or return to the body that gave rise to it, which was my own. It had no images connected with it, and no object but pure physical sensation. It was as if I had found a way of singing that did not come from the throat. I stumbled upon it by accident and it did not cross my mind that anybody might ever have had this experience except me. Therefore I did not connect these piercing exquisite sensations with the act of murder that removed Cletus Smith from Lincoln, or with what other men and women did that was all right for them to do provided they were married. Or even with what older boys talked about in the locker room at school. It was an all but passive, wholly private passion that turned me into two boys, one of whom went to high school and was conscientious about handing in his homework and tried out for the glee club and the debating society and lingered after school talking to his algebra teacher. The other boy was moody and guilt-ridden and desired nothing from other people but their absence.

When I was in bed, with the light out, the two boys became one, and I thought about the aerial on the roof, and how the cold air above our house was full of unknown voices and dance music, from a radio station downtown and from stations in Springfield and Peoria and Bloomington and Danville and Chicago and Kansas City. In college I read Shakespeare's *The Tempest* for the first time and was reminded immediately of what went on over the house in Park Place.

My father was offered a promotion that meant he would work in the Chicago office of the fire insurance company and be home every night like other men. At his age he didn't want to travel from one small town to another and be at the mercy of railroad timetables any more. Also, he was ambitious and gratified that they wanted him. My stepmother could not bear the thought of leaving Lincoln and her family and her friends. Night after night she wept while she and my father talked behind the closed door of their room. After a few years she could say that she preferred living in Chicago, but she was never again as lighthearted as she was before they left Lincoln.

The move to Chicago came in March but I stayed behind to finish the school year. I was taken in by old Mrs. McGrath. Her house had only two bedrooms, and for three months Grace's brother Ted and I slept in his room, in twin four-poster beds. One would have thought that having the company of a schoolboy was the one thing hitherto lacking in his very agreeable life. At night he took off his toupee and hung it on a bedpost, and as we were undressing he imparted his favorite words of wisdom to me, such as "Marriage is what takes the giggles out of the girls," or "You can't make a man mad by giving him money," or "All little things are nice." In the morning before school we all three crowded into the breakfast nook off the kitchen and ate buckwheat cakes and maple syrup. I persisted in feeling that I was putting them to a great deal of trouble when I don't suppose I was, actually.

When it was time for me to go to Chicago, Ted and another of Grace's brothers drove me there, stopping on the way to inspect a gravel pit in Joliet. They checked in at the La Salle Hotel, in Chicago, and we had dinner. As I stood gaping at the coffered ceiling, the like of which I had never seen before, they stuffed ten-dollar bills in my pockets. I didn't know whether it was right for me to take the money or not, and tried not to, but they assured me that it was perfectly all right, my father wouldn't mind, and in the end I took half of it. Instead of using the elevated railway, as I expected, we drove all the way from the Loop to Rogers Park in a taxi so I could see the city. As I looked out of the window at Sheridan Road they looked at me, and were so full of delight in the pleasure they were giving me that some final thread of resistance gave way and I understood not only how entirely generous they were but also that generosity might be the greatest pleasure there is.

Home was now an apartment on the second floor of a three-story brick building. The apartment house was a block west of Sheridan Road, in a quiet neighborhood, and Lake Michigan was only a short walk from where we lived. There were still lots of big old-fashioned single-family houses with front porches and trees and some sort of lawn and a homelike look to them. My father found a job for me in his office as a filing clerk, and he and I went to work together on the El. In the evening the boys used to cluster on the sidewalk with their bicycles and I would walk by them with a dry mouth and my eyes focused on something farther down the street. I usually ended up at the Lake, where I sat on a rock pile looking out over the water. This went on for most of the summer, until one evening I found my way blocked by a bicycle wheel. The boy who was astride the bicycle asked if I was Jewish. It was not anti-Semitism, he was just curious. The circle opened and took me in. I mean, I could stand around with them and nobody objected to my being there.

After Labor Day I started to school. In a city high school of three thousand students, where there was so much going on after school—band practice, fencing, the Stamp Collectors Club, the History Club, the French Club, the Players, the Orchestra, the Camera Club, the Chess and Chequer Club, the Architectural Society, and so on—the failure to do well in sports didn't make you an object of derision. Once in an outdoor gym class a football came through the air and I managed to hang on to it. This was long after the class had stopped expecting me to catch anything and there was general rejoicing and disbelief. But they never rode me. I was accepted for what I was. It was, after all, not a small town but a big city, and in that school there was no one who was not accepted.

The school building was of grey stone and enormous. It was ten times as big as the old, overcrowded, yellow-brick high school in Lincoln, and the classrooms I had to go to were sometimes far apart. One day during the first week or so of school as I was hurrying along a corridor that was lined with metal lockers I saw Cletus Smith coming toward me. It was as if he had risen from the dead. He didn't speak. I didn't speak. We just kept on walking until we had passed each other. And after that, there was no way that I could not have done it.

Why didn't I speak to him? I guess because I was so surprised. And because I didn't know what to say. I didn't know what was polite in the circumstances. I couldn't say *I'm sorry about the murder and all that*, could I? In Greek tragedies, the Chorus never attempts to console the innocent bystander but instead, sticking to broad generalities, grieves over the fate of mankind, whose mistake was to have been born in the first place.

If I had been the elderly man I am now I might have simply said his name. Or shaken my head sadly and said, "I know, I know. . . ." But would that have been any better? I wasn't an elderly man, the bloodhounds had never been after my father, and I didn't know (how could anybody know, how many times has such a thing happened to a thirteen-year-old boy?) what he had been through. Any more than a person who hasn't had a car door slammed on his fingers knows what that is like.

Boys are, from time to time, found hanging from a rafter or killed by a shotgun believed to have gone off accidentally. The wonder is it happens so seldom.

I think now—I think if I had turned and walked along beside him and not said anything, it might have been the right thing to do. But that's what I think *now*. It has taken me all these years even to imagine doing that, and I had a math class on the second floor, clear at the other end of the building, and there was just barely time to get there before the bell rang.

5

The Emotion of Ownership

Until I was six years old, my father kept a carriage horse, and on hot July evenings we would leave the house on Ninth Street and go driving to cool off. Sometimes the couple who lived next door would be invited to go with us. My brother sat in the front seat, between my father and Dr. Donald, and I sat in back, between Mrs. Donald and my mother. The dog—though we all shouted "Go *home!*" at him—went too, trotting between the wheels of the carriage with his tongue lolling out.

No matter what street my father chose to drive out of town by, the landscape was much the same once we got out in the country. Plowed fields or pasture, all the way to the horizon. There were trees for the cattle to stand under in the heat of the day, and the fields were separated from each other by Osage-orange hedgerows that were full of nesting birds.

The conversation in the front seat of the carriage was about what was growing on both sides of the road: corn, wheat, rye, oats, alfalfa. The women, blind to this green wealth, talked about sewing and "receipts"—the word they used for recipes. I was of an age to appreciate anything that looked like something it wasn't, and when we passed a cluster of mailboxes I would turn and look back. Long-legged wading birds is what they put me in the mind of, though we were a considerable distance from anything that could be called a body of water.

Dr. Donald owned land near Mason City. The eighty-acre farm that my father might have inherited had, to his undying regret, been sold by my grandparents. Living carefully and putting aside half his salary, he had managed to buy a farm, but it was a little too far away to drive to in a horse and carriage, and since he couldn't look at his own land, as he would undoubtedly have liked to do, he enjoyed looking at other people's. With a gesture of the whip he would direct Dr. Donald's attention to a large and well-built barn and they would be moved to admiration. By nature home-loving, I looked at the houses instead. How bleak they were, compared to our house in town. No big shade trees, no wide front porch to sit on, no neighbors all up and down the street. If there were flowers they didn't amount to more than a few dusty hollyhocks or some nasturtiums growing in a tin basin on a stump.

Suppose Cletus had come to spend the day with me when we were small children. There would have been a dog following us around. And in the barn a horse, a high carriage with red wheels, hay, bags of oats, etc. But then he would have discovered that I had never harnessed the horse to the carriage, and that we couldn't ride him bareback to round up the cows because there weren't any. The house was a lot larger and more comfortable than his, and there was a sand-pile in the back yard, but what was a sandpile compared to the horse barn, the cow barn, sheds, corncribs, the chicken house, the root cellar, the well, the windmill, the horse trough, and a swimming hole? In town there were cardinals and bluebirds and tanagers and Baltimore orioles, but he had the mourning dove, the forever inquiring bob-*white?*, the hoot owl, and the whippoorwill.

My father sold the horse and carriage and tore down the
barn and built a garage to put the new seven-passenger
Chalmers in, and after that we could drive to Mt. Pulaski,
where his farm was. Tagging around after him then, I became aware of a richness that wasn't visual but came from
the way the smells were laid on: dried-out wood, rusting
farm machinery, the manure pile, the pigpen, yarrow, and
onion grass, quicklime from the outhouse, in spring the
frost leaving the ground, in summer the hay lying cut in the
fields. All things considered, I doubt very much if Cletus
would have been eager to change places with me.

The black fertile soil of Logan County was, and so far as
I know still is, owned by people whose ancestors came from
Kentucky or Indiana or Ohio, bringing with them no more
than they could fit into a lurching covered wagon. They
staked out as much land as they had a fancy to and cleared
it slowly, putting a few more acres under cultivation each
year. Their children and grandchildren, born on this land,
felt they belonged there. Their great-grandchildren either
sold their patrimony or got someone else to farm it for them.
Living in town quite comfortably in big old houses set well
back from the street, they kept an eye on what was going
on out in the country, and when the crops were delivered
at the grain elevator they took, as was customary, half the
profits. They did not consider a tenant farmer their social
equal, any more than a carpenter or a stonemason or a
bricklayer. The farmer who owned the land he farmed they
could and did accept. When Cletus and I were playing together the question of social position didn't come up. And
neither did it come up on the school playground. It was
something that descended upon people when they were
older. The names on the mailboxes that claimed my attention when I was a small child were proof enough that the
tenant farmers were of the same stock as the townspeople

who looked down on them socially. Their forebears had perhaps come on a later wave of European migration and found that land was no longer plentiful at a dollar and a quarter an acre. Or they could have been hamstrung by some family misfortune. Or simply lacked the talent for rising in the world.

Roaming the courthouse square on a Saturday night, the tenant farmers and their families were unmistakable. You could see that they were not at ease in town and that they clung together for support. The women's clothes were not meant to be becoming but to wear well, to last them out. The back of the men's necks was a mahogany color, and deeply wrinkled. Their hands were large and looked swollen or misshapen and sometimes they were short a finger or two. The discontented hang of their shoulders is possibly something I imagined because I would not have liked not owning the land I farmed. Very likely they didn't either, but farming was in their blood and they wouldn't have cared to be selling real estate or adding up columns of figures in a bank.

On the seventh day they rested; that is to say, they put on their good clothes and hitched up the horse again and drove to some country church, where, sitting in straight-backed cushionless pews, they stared passively at the preacher, who paced up and down in front of them, thinking up new ways to convince them that they were steeped in sin.

If I knew where Cletus Smith is right this minute, I would go and explain. Or try to. It is not only possible but more than likely that I would also have to explain who I am. And that he would have no recollection of the moment that has troubled me all these years. He lived through things that were a good deal worse. It might turn out that I had made the effort for my sake, not his.

I don't know where he is. It isn't at all likely that we will run into each other somewhere or that we would recognize each other if we did. He could even be dead.

Except through the intervention of chance, the one possibility of my making some connection with him seems to lie not in the present but in the past—in my trying to reconstruct the testimony that he was never called upon to give. The unsupported word of a witness who was not present except in imagination would not be acceptable in a court of law, but, as it has been demonstrated over and over, the sworn testimony of the witness who was present is not trustworthy either. If any part of the following mixture of truth and fiction strikes the reader as unconvincing, he has my permission to disregard it. I would be content to stick to the facts if there were any.

The reader will also have to do a certain amount of imagining. He must imagine a deck of cards spread out face down on a table, and then he must turn one over, only it is not the eight of hearts or the jack of diamonds but a perfectly ordinary quarter of an hour out of Cletus's past life. But first I need to invent a dog, which doesn't take very much in the way of prestidigitation; if there were cattle there had to be a dog to help round them up. In that period—I don't know how it is now—farm dogs were usually a mixture of collie and English shepherd. The attraction between dogs and adolescent boys can, I think, be taken for granted. There is no outward sign of trouble in the family. The two farms are both on the right-hand side of the new hard road and have a common boundary line. The Wilson house, with its barns and sheds, is next to the road and an eighth of a mile closer to town. To get to where Cletus lives you have to drive up a narrow lane that has a gate at either end of it.

When it is almost time for Cletus to come home from school the dog squeezes herself under the gates and trots off up the road to the mailboxes, where she settles down in a place that she has made for herself in the high grass with her chin resting on her four paws. These mailboxes too are on posts and look like wading birds.

In the very few years since my father disposed of the horse and carriage, there has been a change in the landscape. It is now like a tabletop, the trees mostly gone, the hedges uprooted in favor of barbed wire—resulting in more land under cultivation, more money in the bank, but also in a total exposure. Anyone can see what used to be reserved for the eye of the hawk as it wheeled in slow circles.

If a farm wagon or a Model T Ford goes by, the dog follows it with her eyes but she does not raise her head. She is expecting a boy on a bicycle.

The tenant farmers whose names are on those mailboxes where the dog lies waiting for Cletus to come home from school apply the words of the Scriptures to their own lives, insofar as they are able. Including the commandment to do unto others as you would have them do unto you. And they cling together when they are in town largely because they cannot imagine a situation in which the people they see in the stores or on the sidewalk (and who do not appear to see them) could possibly need their help. It is different in the country.

The bicycle is painted a bright blue, and Cletus has only had it for three months. When he first saw it, beside the Christmas tree, his heart almost stopped beating. On rainy days he walks to school rather than have it get old and rusty like the other bikes in the wooden rack at the side of the one-room schoolhouse. With the dog loping along beside him he pedals for dear life over the final stretch of road. The dog waits each time until he has closed the gate and then she trots on ahead importantly, as if by himself the boy wouldn't know the way home. Scratching hens have destroyed the grass in the farmyard, and the house could do with a coat of paint, but the roof doesn't leak and the barns are not about to fall down. The dog follows Cletus up onto the porch, leaving her neat footprints wherever she has been. With her head cocked she watches while he puts his schoolbooks beside the door and bends down to untie his shoelaces. His head is now on a level with hers. The plumed tail wags seductively. He leans forward so that she can smell his breath and, smelling hers, wrinkles his nose with distaste.

"Whew! What have you been eating? Dead fish?" Dead something.

There is no telling how long she would let him go on looking into her agate-colored eyes. Forever, possibly. She has made him a present of herself and nothing he does or doesn't do will make her take it back. "Good dog," he says, and steps out of his shoes. The dog knows better than to try and sneak into the house with him, but that doesn't mean she likes being kept out. She withdraws her long, pointed, sensitive nose an inch at a time, allowing the door to close. Then she whines softly, inviting him to relent.

Let us consider the kitchen the dog is not allowed into. Steam on the windows. Zinc surfaces that have lost their shine. Wooden surfaces that have been scrubbed to the texture of velvet. The range, with two buckets of water beside it ready to be poured into the reservoir when it is empty. The teakettle. The white enamel coffeepot. The tin matchbox on the wall. The woodbox, the sink, the comb hanging by a string, the roller towel. The kerosene lamp with a white glass shade. The embossed calendar. The kitchen chairs, some with a crack in the seat. The cracked oilcloth on the kitchen table. The smell of Octagon soap. To the indifferent eye it is like every farm kitchen for a hundred miles around, but none of those others would have been waiting in absolute stillness for Cletus to come home from school, or have seemed like all his heart desired when he walks in out of the cold.

When Cletus stands by the pasture fence, an old white workhorse comes, expecting a lump of sugar and possibly hoping to be loved. Anyway, Cletus loves him. And, rounding up the cows, rides him in preference to any of the other horses. And when he has tears to shed he does it with his forehead against the horse's silky neck.

In the daytime the sky is an inverted bowl over the prairie. On a clear night it is sometimes powdered with stars.

Coming home from school Cletus often sees Mrs. Wilson and the two little boys out by the clothesline. Risking a fall he takes both hands off the handlebars and waves, and they wave back.

It is not by accident that Cletus is often in the Wilsons' buggy when the two families drive off to church together or to town to see the fireworks on the Fourth of July. They are his second family. If his mother sends him to the Wilsons' because she has suddenly discovered that she is out of vanilla or allspice, there is a good chance that Mrs. Wilson will cut a slice off a loaf of bread that has just come out of the oven and spread butter and jam on it and give it to him. He likes her apart from that, though; he likes her because she is always the same.

When it was time for him to go to school the Wilson girls showed him the shortcut through the fields to the other road and the one-room schoolhouse, and Hazel had to tell the teacher his name. With all those strange boys and girls staring at him he lost the power of speech. The teacher was young and pretty and showed him how to hold the colored crayon.

If Cletus wants to know something and his father isn't

there to show him, he goes looking for Mr. Wilson. Who doesn't lose patience with him if he fails to get it right on the first try. When Mr. Wilson says to Cletus's father, "I saw a cock pheasant crossing the road this morning, I don't suppose you feel like taking the afternoon off to go hunting," it is understood that, providing it isn't a school day, Cletus will go with them. His mother was afraid and wanted him to wait until he was older but Mr. Wilson said, "Better for him to learn now, while he hasn't got a lot of other things in his mind. . . . Here, boy. You hold it like this. With the stock against your right shoulder. And you keep both eyes open and sight along the barrel to that bead. If you obey the rules that your father tells you and don't go out with some fool who's never had a shotgun in his hand before, you can't get into trouble."

Sometimes he rests his hand on Cletus's shoulder while he is talking. At such moments Cletus feels that no matter what he might do, even if it was something quite bad that he had to go to jail for, Mr. Wilson would see a reason for it. And stand by him. Not that his father wouldn't also, but Mr. Wilson is somebody Cletus isn't even related to.

In that flat landscape a man cursing at his horses somewhere off in the fields can be heard a long way. All sounds carry: the dinner bell, wheels crossing a cattle guard, the clatter of farm machinery. When the gasoline engine sputters and dies or the blades of the mowing machine jam, Cletus knows that Mr. Wilson, a quarter of a mile away, has heard it and is waiting for the sound of the engine or the mowing machine to start up again. If it doesn't, he leaves his own work and comes across the pasture to see what the trouble is. With their heads almost touching, his father and Mr. Wilson study the difficulty. Wrenches and pliers pass back and forth between them with as much familiarity as if they owned their four hands in common.

In midsummer, with thunderheads blotting out more and more of the blue sky, it could be his father's hay that they are tossing up onto the wain or it could be Mr. Wilson's. They know, of course, but it is beside the point. When the haymakers no longer cast a shadow it means that the sun has gone under a huge, ominous, dark grey cloud. A breeze springs up and they work faster. They don't even so much as glance at the sky. They don't need to. The precariously balanced load grows higher and higher. When the wagon won't hold any more they climb up onto it and race for the barn, and with the first raindrops pattering on the oak leaves they congratulate themselves on getting the hay under cover in time. This happens not just once but year after year.

So far as Clarence Smith was concerned, no other man had ever shown a concern so genuine or so dependable, and he did his best to pay it back in kind. When Lloyd Wilson had a sick calf, instead of calling the vet he got Clarence to come and look at it, and Clarence stayed up all night doctoring the animal and keeping it warm with blankets. In the morning Cletus woke up early and threw the covers off and dressed and ran all the way to the barn where they were, and got there in time to see the calf struggle to his feet. His father said, "I guess that's that," and brushed Mr. Wilson's thanks aside, and they went home.

And when his father gets behind in his spring plowing because of the rains, Mr. Wilson joins him after supper with his horse and plow and together they turn over the soil in the lower forty by moonlight.

Cletus thinks of it as their lower forty; actually, it is someone else's. Land, barns, sheds, farmhouse—everything but livestock and machinery—belong to Colonel Dowling, whose snub-nosed Franklin is often parked by the entrance to the lane. The crops that are planted and the price at which they are sold await his decision. The lightning rods on the roof of the house and both barns are his idea. It is right, of course, to put your trust in the Lord. But in moderation. Things that people can manage without His help He shouldn't be asked to take care of. After the time the Franklin got so badly mired in the lane that his tenant had to come with a team and pull him out, Colonel Dowling doesn't put his entire trust in the Franklin either, but tells himself it is just as easy to leave the car by the side of the road and walk in.

He is a self-made man. His father was a hod carrier who drank more than was good for him, and fell off a scaffolding and broke his neck, leaving his widow with six children to bring up. She did it by taking in washing. As Ed Dowling fought his way up in the world, he married a woman with money and made himself into a gentleman. It was no small accomplishment, but it cut him off somewhat from his brothers and sisters, who are not above making fun of him behind his back.

A gentleman doesn't have one set of manners for the house of a poor man and another for the house of someone with an income comparable to his own. He never enters the farmhouse without knocking. Even though it is legally his. And he remembers to wipe the spring mud off his shoes. He also makes a point of asking Cletus's mother if she is satisfied with the present arrangements, and this could lead to, if she thinks the kitchen needs repainting, his offering to supply the paint. He is always courteous to her and he knows the boys' names. If that is all he knows about them, it is not greatly to be wondered at. One farm boy is very much like another. The cat has invariably got their tongue.

Satisfied that his tenant's wife is a good housekeeper, he shows no interest in the second floor, and therefore doesn't know about the broken-backed copy of *Tom Swift and His Flying Machine* that is lying open, with the pages to the floor, in the fluff under the bed in the small room on the right at the head of the stairs.

Colonel Dowling is older than Cletus's father, and has snow-white hair, and Cletus finds it natural that when they stand talking by the pump or when they walk over the fields together his father calls the older man "Colonel" and Colonel Dowling calls his father "Clarence." But sometimes the Colonel brings a friend with him, somebody from town who doesn't know the first thing about farming, and with Cletus's father standing right there he will say "my corn" or "my oats" or "my drainage ditch." If he says it often enough, Cletus drops behind out of earshot. Even if his father, after working these acres for twelve years, doesn't feel the emotion of ownership, Cletus does.

Another card, from that same pack: his brother Wayne, who is eight years younger than he is. Wayne and Cletus are as different as day and night, people say. Or, to put it differently, as different as the oldest child and the second one often are.

Watching his mother as she holds Wayne's chin in her hand and parts his hair with a wet comb, Cletus remembers that she used to do this to him.

All the way home from school there are clouds racing across the sky and the air is warm and humid. Wayne is sitting on the porch steps when Cletus rides into the yard. He has pulled a strawberry box apart and is making an airplane with the pieces of thin wood. As Cletus steps over him he bends down and tries to take it from him in order to make an improvement, but Wayne jerks it back.

"Aunt Jenny is here," he says. "Somebody gave her a ride out from town. And we're having strawberry shortcake for supper."

Except for Jenny Evans, who is her mother's sister, Fern Smith has no living relatives. Her mother died when she was three and her father gave her to Aunt Jenny to bring up and went out West, where he found a job on a cattle ranch in Wyoming. From time to time he sent money, never very much. Now he is dead too. So is Tom Evans, Jenny's husband.

As people get older they get more alike in character and appearance and could all be leading the same life. Or almost. Shut up in the little house opposite the fairgrounds, Aunt Jenny talks to the hot-water faucet that drips, and the kitchen drawer that has a tendency to stick. She also sings, hymns mostly, in a high quavering voice: "That Old Rugged Cross" and "Art Thou Weary, Art Thou Sad" and "How glorious must the mansions be / Where thy redeemed shall dwell with thee. . . ." Without meaning to, she has grown heavy but she eats so little that short of starving to death there doesn't seem much she can do about it. Sometimes she goes out to work as a practical nurse, and comes home and sits by the kitchen table soaking her feet in a pan of hot water and Epsom salts. When she gets into bed and the springs creak under her weight, she groans with the pleasure of lying stretched out on an object that understands her so well.

The face that passes in and out of the small unframed mirror over the kitchen sink is that of an old woman whose chin has hairs on it, whose teeth spent the night in a glass of water, whose glasses are bifocal, causing her to step down into space if she isn't careful. She is full of fears, which are nursed by the catastrophes she reads about in the paper. The front and back doors are locked day and night against bad boys, a man with a mask over the lower part of his face, pneumonia, a fall. There is, even so, something buoyant in her nature that makes people pleased to see her coming toward them on the street, and usually they stop to talk to her and hear about the catastrophes. She winds up the conversation by saying cheerfully, "Life is no joke." What sensible person wouldn't agree with her.

The house is her one great accomplishment. Against all odds she has managed to hang on to it. "It's a poor man's house," she loves to say, "and not much to look at." It doesn't do to brag about your possessions, especially to people who have less. The mortgage is paid off and she doesn't have to take in roomers. It is all hers—meaning the pollarded catalpa tree by the front sidewalk, the woodshed around in back, the outside sloping cellar door, and the porch light that doesn't turn on. Meaning also the white net curtains that have turned grey and are about ready for the ragbag, the nine-by-twelve linoleum rug in the front room, with the design worn completely away in places, the ugly golden-oak furniture that could be duplicated in any secondhand store, "Sir Galahad" and "The Dickey Bird," and the smell of the kerosene heater. The two upstairs rooms are hot in summer and expensive to heat in winter, and so she doesn't use them. The big double bed all but blocking the front door makes the front room look queer, but she has stopped caring what people think. She means to die here, in her own house, in this very bed.

Meanwhile, she is not alone in the world. From the fairgrounds to the first fence post of the farm is a little over a mile, and when Aunt Jenny is feeling blue she puts on her hat and coat and, armed with grape jelly or a jar of pickles, pays them a visit. She tries not to come too often and she is careful never to take sides between husband and wife. Blessed is the peacemaker for he shall—inherit the kingdom of heaven? . . . see God? She can't remember, offhand, and keeps meaning to open the Bible to Matthew 5, and see which it is. Clarence is kind to her and brings her fruit and vegetables that she cans and lives on all winter. Fern is in the habit of leaving Wayne with her when she goes to the stores. And used to do the same thing with Cletus when he was small.

"Come and give your old auntie a kiss," she says now when Cletus appears in the doorway. "I know you don't like to kiss people but it won't kill you, not this once."

"It's going to rain," he says, and either his mother doesn't hear him or else she failed to connect what he has just said with the washing on the line. He goes on upstairs and takes off his school clothes and hangs them on an already over-crowded hook. The room gets progressively darker as the rainstorm that is moving across the prairie approaches.

Even in the dead of winter, the only heat there ever is in this room comes through the ventilator in the floor. Voices also are carried by it. Though he can hear the conversation in the room below, he manages not to understand it. What sounds like somebody moving furniture around is the first thunder, faint and far away.

The water in the china pitcher comes from the cistern and is rainwater and rust-colored. He fills the bowl and the water immediately turns cloudy from the soap and dirt on his hands. From the room below he hears "Fortunately I have witnesses."

Him, among others. She has—his mother has fits of weeping in the night. The walls are thin. Lying awake, he hears threats he tries not to believe and accusations he doesn't understand. And envies the dog, who can put her head on her paws and go to sleep when she doesn't like the way things are.

Raindrops spatter against the windowpane and he turns

and looks out. The tops of the trees are swaying in the wind. The sky behind the windmill is a greenish almost-black, and his mother and Aunt Jenny, with their coats over their heads, are yanking the sheets from the line. There is a flash of lightning that makes everything in sight turn pale, and then deep rolling thunder.

He goes on soaping his hands slowly, lost in a daydream about a motorcycle he has seen in the Sears, Roebuck catalogue.

As Aunt Jenny is drawn toward the farm, so the hired man, Victor Jensen, feels the pull of town. Bright and early on the morning of Decoration Day he gets dressed up fit to kill and starts off down the highway. The same thing happens on the Fourth of July and Labor Day. Though they know what he is heading for, they do not make any effort to stop him. It is his reward for not belonging to anybody and not having anybody who belongs to him. He isn't home by milking time, and they know then that he won't come home at all. In the morning when they go to his room in the barn his bed has not been slept in. Various neighbors report that they have seen him in town—during the parade, or on the courthouse square, or at the band concert, reeling. Two days later, a buggy drives up the lane and stops. Cletus comes to the door and Lloyd Wilson says, "I passed Victor on the road just now. He was headed in this direction and I tried to get him to climb in with me but he wouldn't. I thought you'd like to know." Cletus and his father go out looking for the hired man and find him lying in a ditch a quarter of a mile from home, and put him to bed in his room in the barn. Except for the stench of alcohol on his breath and the dried vomit on his clothes, it is like undressing a child. The next day he is up in time to help with the chores. He is deathly pale and his hands shake. Nobody mentions his absence and he is not apologetic—just withdrawn. As if he had answered a summons and is in no way responsible for what followed.

Another card: the cats run to greet Cletus when he walks into the barn. His father is already there, milking Flossie, and Victor is milking the new cow. "Sorry I'm late," Cletus says and picks up a milk bucket and a stool and sits down beside Old Bess, and then there are three of them going squirt-squirt, in approximately the same rhythm. He isn't as good a milker as his father, but nobody is. When his father was Cletus's age he was milking fifteen cows morning and night. The level of the milk rises slowly in the pails, and Old Bess manages to hit him in the eye with her tail, as usual.

"I thought I told you to come straight home from school."

"Teacher kept me."

"You been causing trouble?"

"I had to stay and make up an arithmetic test. I flunked it the first time."

"Not what I send you to school for."

"I know."

If Cletus didn't go to school at all he wouldn't care. It is the way things are here that matters. He can't grow up fast enough. When he is grown, there won't be anything his father can do that he can't do.

He is sitting at the kitchen table with his head bent over his arithmetic. He puts the end of his lead pencil in his mouth frequently so the numbers will be black instead of grey. The darkness outside presses against the windowpanes here also, but they are too accustomed to this to notice it.

"I must go home," Mr. Wilson says, and doesn't.

Except for the chores, all farming is at a standstill. Snow lies deep on the ground and in much deeper drifts wherever it met with an obstruction. The wooden fence posts and the well roof are capped, and icicles hang from the gutters.

His father and Mr. Wilson are talking about the relative merits of clover and alfalfa as a cover crop. Cletus would like to follow this conversation but there are twelve problems and he has only done half of them. "What's nine times seven?" he asks his mother, who tells him and then rests her chin on Wayne's curls and utters the single word "Bedtime." Wayne wants Cletus to go upstairs with him.

"Why does he have to be such a baby? There's nothing upstairs that is going to hurt him."

"Oh, be nice and go with him. You were afraid of the dark once. You just don't remember."

So he closes his book and gets up from the table, though he hasn't finished the assignment and Teacher will probably be sore at him.

Teacher wasn't sore at him, as it turned out. She knows he is a gentle boy and tries hard.

The rain is drumming on the tin roof of the shed off the kitchen where the separator is, and where Cletus's mother makes them keep their work shoes so they won't track the barnyard mud and manure into the house. He ties his shoelaces and makes a dash for it, with the dog bounding at his heels. When they arrive at the horse barn his hair is plastered to his head and his shirt is sticking to his back. The dog gets as close to him as she can and then shakes herself.

"Thanks. How'd you like it if I did that to you?"

He doesn't really hold it against her and she doesn't look guilty. They both know it is just something she has to do because she is a dog. It is warm and dry in the barn and he soon stops shivering. He cleans out the stalls and puts down fresh hay for the horses and fills the water buckets, all the while enjoying the sight of the rain coming down on the plowed field beyond the open door.

In the night he gives Wayne a poke and says, "Move over, you're crowding me out of bed." Sometimes Cletus jabbers in his sleep. Mostly they lie curled together in what is not a very large bed sleeping the sleep of stones. The north wind howling around the corner of the house only serves to deepen this unknowing.

Dressing for church Clarence Smith puts on a clean white shirt and discovers that Fern hasn't washed his collars. And is angry with her. He has his duties to perform and she has hers, one of which is to see that he has clean clothes to put on.

The small country church is packed with his neighbors, all of whom are wearing clean collars. The giving out of the hymn number causes them to rise and add the droning of their country voices to the wheezing of the little organ. Since the preacher said that the point of the parables is mysterious and needs explaining, they have no choice but to believe him. The details—the great supper, the lost lamb, the unproductive vineyard, the unjust steward, the sower, and the seed sown secretly—they are familiar with and understand. Above the transparent dome they live and work under there is another even grander where they will reside in mansions waiting to receive them when they are done with farming forever.

What Clarence Smith sees as he helps his wife into the

front seat of the buggy after church is a woman who in the sight of God is his lawfully wedded wife and owes him love, honor, and obedience. Other people, with nothing at stake, see that there is a look of sadness about her, as if she lives too much in the past or perhaps expects more of life than is reasonable.

6

Lloyd Wilson's Story

Though he had brothers he was on good terms with, the person he turned to for companionship or when he had something weighing on his mind was the overserious man on the neighboring farm. After twelve years he found it hard to believe there had ever been a time when he and Clarence weren't friends. At night, in the immense darkness, the only light he could see came from the Smiths' house.

He remembered the day they came. A raw, wet, windy day in March. He was plowing next to the road when he saw an unfamiliar wagon piled high with stuff drive up the lane at Colonel Dowling's, and he threw the reins over the horse's neck and started across the fields. When he got to the house, the front door was unlocked and standing open but the new neighbors were still outside, looking around to see where they were—the man a little under average height, and a young woman with a baby. They'd been on the road since daybreak. They couldn't have been thirty yet, either of them, but already there were wrinkles in the man's forehead and at the corners of his eyes. His voice was low, and if he could indicate something by a gesture instead of speech, he did. And what crossed Lloyd Wilson's mind was how defenseless he seemed.

Saying "Easy . . . easy . . . now your side . . . a little

more . . . more . . . a little more," the two men maneuvered
a heavy wardrobe up the stairs and through a narrow doorway. You didn't have to be much of a judge of character to
see that the woman had been hoping for something better
and the man was being patient with her. She didn't seem to
know what to do first. Brought up in town, he said to himself. And then, noticing how small her wrists were: "Here,
ma'am, let me have that. It's too heavy for a woman to
carry." As he handled their furniture and their crockery,
and box after box of possessions they hadn't been able to
part with, he found out things about them, that first day,
that it would have taken him years to discover under ordinary circumstances. Poking the baby's stomach gently with
his forefinger, he produced a smile. "Two of my own," he
said as he turned away. He came upon the woman standing
forlornly in the midst of a kitchen that had been stripped
of everything, including the stove, and said, "My wife is expecting you folks for supper." She wasn't, but no matter.
And anyways, they knew she couldn't be expecting them
because nobody knew they were coming. When the others
sat down to eat, Fern nursed her baby in the rocking chair in
the parlor. Afterward, he walked the new neighbors back
to their house and waited till they had lit the lamps.

In the county clerk's platbook the hundred and sixty acres
that Lloyd Wilson farmed were listed as belonging to Mrs.
Mildred Stroud. It did not trouble him, or at least it did not
trouble him very much, that the cows were his and the grass
they cropped was not. The rent he had to pay on the pasture
acreage was not unreasonable. His father had had the place
before him and had saved up enough money over the years
so that when his health failed and he had to give up farming
he could live out his days in town.

Mrs. Stroud was a woman in her early fifties with two unmarried daughters who lived at home and were kept in the dark about her financial affairs, as she had been kept in the dark about her husband's—until he died suddenly and the president of the bank began to explain things to her. He started in as though speaking to a child and then had to pull himself up short. It had been his fixed opinion that all women are ignorant about money matters, but this woman didn't happen to be, and the questions she put to him were just the questions he would have preferred not to answer. It was quite impossible to take advantage of her. Inadvertent mistakes didn't escape her notice either. Like most extremely clever people, she underestimated the intelligence of others. She could have remarried and chose not to because it would have meant discussing what she did with her money.

She appeared at her farm frequently and without giving her tenant any warning. If she did that, what would have been the point in her coming? When she pitched into Lloyd Wilson for some piece of slackness, he cleared his throat and moistened his lips, as if he was about to argue with her, but instead he turned away, pretending that something a few feet to the right or left of them had engaged his attention at that moment. At other times, cap in hand, he was overly polite, in a way that could be taken for rudeness, but this she simply ignored. She knew, because she had made it her business to know everything about him, that if he hadn't got his corn in by the time he should have it was probably because he was off planting somebody else's corn —some neighbor who, because of sickness or whatever, wasn't able to do it himself. She could have made an issue of this and didn't. In the end her corn got planted and she was never actually out of pocket. It was the principle of the thing that she objected to. As her tenant his first responsibility ought to be to her. If she didn't like the way he farmed she could ask him to leave and put some other tenant on the place instead, but they both knew that this wasn't about to happen.

The secret that Mildred Stroud managed to keep from him, though not from herself, was that she found him physically attractive. But she was fifteen years older than he was, and, knowing the cruelty of Lincoln gossip, didn't choose to be the subject of it. And anyway it was out of the question.

Chewing on a grass blade, he remarked—this was in the days when he and Clarence were still friends and he could say whatever came into his head, knowing it wouldn't be repeated or misunderstood—"A good wife is a woman who is always tired, suffers from backache and headaches, and moves away from her husband in bed because she doesn't want any more children." And Clarence supposed that it wasn't just any good wife he was speaking of.

What Lloyd Wilson didn't say (because there was nothing anybody could do about it anyway and why should he burden Clarence with his trouble, if you could call it that) was that he didn't seem capable any more of the kind of feelings he used to have. He was perfectly aware of his wife's good qualities. She worked like a slave, from morning till night, holding up her end of things. She was a good mother. There was no question about any of this. Sometimes he thought it was just that they were so used to each other. He knew how she felt about almost everything, and, most of the time, what she was going to say before she said it. If they had been brother and sister it wouldn't have been very different—except that she was jealous. If he so much as looked at another woman she acted as if he'd done something unforgivable. Once or twice she worked herself up to such a pitch that she went upstairs and started packing. He knew that such persuasion as he could muster was half-hearted and wouldn't convince her to change her mind. If she was bent on leaving him there was nothing he could do about it. She didn't leave him, she only threatened to. None of those women meant anything to him, he said. And with her face averted she said, "The trouble is, I don't mean anything to you either."

Whether he himself would have come to this conclusion if she hadn't embarrassed him by putting it into words, he couldn't say. All he knew was that he wished she hadn't said it. He was ready to provide for her and to treat her with respect, but he couldn't work up a semblance of the emotion that would have made her happy.

Between these crises they lived like any other married couple. You could not have told from her voice as she said, "I'm about to put things on the table, Lloyd," or his voice as he said, "Pass the salt and pepper, please," that there was anything wrong.

He wondered if other men felt the same way about their wives or if it was just him. He was almost forty years old and lately it had seemed to him that he had lived a long time and that just about everything that could happen to him had happened.

When his evening chores were done he walked over the hill and, leaning against a post in the cow barn, directed a steady stream of conversation at the back of Clarence's head. When Clarence and Victor carried the milk to the shed off the kitchen where the separator was, he followed them. And from there into the house. Anything to keep from going home. Sometimes he told himself he ought not to go to the Smiths' so often. He was afraid of becoming a nuisance, and still not quite able to stay away. One night, sitting

in their kitchen, he tried to tell them how much their friendship meant to him, and then broke off in embarrassment,
because anything he might say seemed so much less than he
felt.

"You don't have to tell us," Fern said, smiling at him.
"And anyway, it isn't as one-sided as you appear to think."
Then she changed the subject.

He sat back, glad that he had spoken and glad she had
stopped him from going on. He also recognized that what
she said wasn't just politeness. They were themselves in front
of him, as if he had assured them (he hadn't, but it was
nevertheless true) that he didn't expect them to be anything
they weren't. All this was altered irrevocably by a change
in him so unexpected that it was as if it had happened without his knowing a thing about it. And after that he could
not go on being natural in front of them.

He said silently (but nevertheless wanting to be heard)
Clarence, you ought not to trust me . . . half expecting
Clarence to answer *Why not?* If Clarence had, then he
would have said *Because all my life I've been a stranger to
myself.*

He hated himself for being weak, for having no will, but
it wasn't that he didn't try to overcome the feelings he
knew he shouldn't have. Time after time he thought he had
overcome them, and it always turned out that he hadn't.
Excuses to pay a visit to the barns (where she wouldn't be,
so there was no harm in it) or to the house (where she
would be) occurred to him constantly. He would reject
four in a row and find himself hurriedly acting on the fifth.
His feet took him there, without his consent. He might as
well have given in in the first place.

Searching for a clue to her feelings, he was alert to the
quality of her voice when she spoke to her children or

Clarence. He knew when she was depressed. He knew also that like most married people she and Clarence quarreled sometimes. Did he imagine it or was it true that they got on better with each other and were more cheerful when he was around?

If he did what he knew he ought to do, which was not go there any more, Clarence would wonder why. So would she. The idea that she would think of him at all pleased him. All day long he thought about her. The cows sensed that he hardly knew what he was doing and turned their heads as far as their stanchions would permit and looked at him gravely.

He sighed, and then a moment later sighed again—deep sighs that seemed to come from as far down as they could come. To have escaped from that deadness, from the feeling that all he had to look forward to was more of the same . . .

But he was careful. He didn't make a simple remark without rehearsing it beforehand. And he continually removed the expression from his face lest it be the wrong one, and give him away. He also avoided any strong light, such as the lamp on the kitchen table. Sometimes a weakness overcame him, his legs were unstrung, and he had to find some place to sit down, but this was easy enough to disguise. It was his voice that gave him the most trouble. It sounded false to him and not like his voice at all.

His wife yawned and then yawned again a minute later, and put the cover on her workbasket and gathered up her mending. "I declare, it's snowing," she said. She got up and went into the bedroom, and he sat looking at the snow, which was coming down in big cottony flakes.

"Aren't you coming, Lloyd?"

He turned the wick down until the lamp sputtered and
went out. Then he went into the next room and, sitting on
the edge of the bed, began to undress. *As long as she doesn't
know how I feel about her* . . .
He kissed her eyelids.

"Now, why would you want to do a thing like that?"
Clarence asked.

"Well, land is cheap, for one thing. I could own my own
farm and raise what I pleased on it, and not have to share
the profits."

"Or the losses, in a bad year. You've been on the Stroud
place all your life. It's home to you. You know everybody
for miles around and they know you. If you get into trouble, you can expect help."

"True enough," Lloyd Wilson said soberly. He knew that
if Clarence did not say "help from me" it was because he
didn't want to remind him how beholden he was.

"Who knows what it is like in Iowa. You may find that
people are friendly out there and then again they may
not be."

What Fern felt, he could not make out. Nothing,
maybe. Maybe she resented his friendship with Clarence and
would be glad if he moved away.

She was standing at the stove, with an apron on, rinsing
the supper dishes in a pan of hot water. She had moved the
lamp to a shelf higher than her head and the light fell on
the nape of her neck, the place that in women and small
children always seemed to express their vulnerability. Looking at the soft blond hairs that had escaped from the comb,
he thought of all those people who, because of their reli-
gion, had knelt down in great perturbation of mind and had

their heads chopped off. His heart was flooded with love for her and he lost the thread of what Clarence was saying.

Riding into town with him, Clarence said, "Fern's as cross as a bear this morning."

"Yes," he said, trying to seem no more interested than if Clarence had said he had to replace some part in the manure spreader.

"I wish I knew what's eating her."

"Maybe nothing. Maybe she's just tired or doesn't feel well."

"Maybe."

"In any case, I doubt if she's the only woman in Logan County that's as cross as a bear this morning."

"There's no pleasing her sometimes," Clarence said, and there the conversation ended. But it had opened up vistas of hope, where before there had been none.

Parting the slit in the front of his underwear, he sent his urine in an arch out onto the frozen ground. It glittered in the moonlight. He was in the shadow of the porch roof, where he could not be seen by anybody driving past—though who would be, before daylight? With one knee bent and his foot braced against the porch railing he stood staring off into the darkness where she was. A minute passed, and then another. The first cock crowed, even though the light in the east hadn't changed. At his back a woman's voice said, "Lloyd, what on earth are you doing out there?" and he turned and went into the house.

He thought his secret was safe until one day when he walked into the kitchen and asked, "Where's Clarence?" and she said coldly, "Why do you keep up this pretense of friendship any longer when you don't like us the way you used to?"

He was dumfounded, and started to defend himself, and then broke off. If he didn't say what was on his heart now he might as well crawl into a hole somewhere and die. His life wouldn't be worth living. . . .

Out it came. Everything. Pouring out of him. He expected to be driven from the house and instead she looked at him the way she looked at her children when they were upset over something—as if, as a human being, he had a right to his feelings, whatever they were. When he took her in his arms she neither accepted his kiss nor resisted it.

Instinct told him that it would end badly.

For a week they avoided each other and accident kept bringing them face to face when there was nobody else around. Each time, they turned away without saying a word, without even touching each other. And got in deeper and deeper. He knew he should be sorry but he was not. Which didn't keep him from grieving for the best friend he had ever had. As if Clarence had met with an accident.

The flood of feeling that informed his heart was like nothing he had ever experienced. If his wife, lying with her back to him on the far side of the bed, knew he was awake she did not show it. Reassured by the sound of her breathing, he lit a match and looked to see what time it was. He had never before not been able to fall asleep the minute his head hit the pillow. Now hour after hour went by and he felt no need for sleep. He felt as if he had just been born.

He lay on his side for a while and then turned, trying not to produce an upheaval in the bed. If things had been differ-

ent, if they'd met when they were young, before Clarence
had come along and . . . He turned again. He was in the
habit of going to his father when he had a problem to deal
with that was totally beyond his experience. He went to his
father now and said *What am I going to do?* And his father
said *Stay on this side of the boundary line till you get over it.*
Good enough advice but if he didn't get over it? This question his father did not seem to want to answer. But he knew
also that if his father had come up with a solution he
wouldn't have been interested. He turned again so that he
was lying on his back, and tears of gratitude ran down his
face, past his ears, through the stubble on his jaw, and
were soaked up by the pillowcase, which smelled of sunshine. . . .

The alarm clock went off and ran all the way down and
he didn't move. Sleep, when it finally came, had felled him.
His wife shook him awake and he was under the impression
that he answered her, but all he did was sit up in bed and
reach for the matches and light the lamp to dress by. Shak-
ing the grates in the kitchen stove he was aware, suddenly,
of how cut off they now were from everybody. And committed to lying.

There was nothing to be done about it. He didn't want
to not love her. It was as simple as that. And with the lantern
swinging from his hand he went off into the darkness as on
any other morning—as he did on the last morning of his
life.

Clarence and the hired man started to carry the full milk
pails into the shed where the separator was, and when he
didn't follow them Clarence turned and said, "Aren't you
coming?"

"Not tonight," he said, only to have his excuses brushed aside.

The memory of making love lay like a bandage across the front of his mind, day and night.

He waited for her to tell him where they would meet, and when. And marveled at the excuses she thought up to get to him. No matter what the excuse was, it always worked. No excuse at all worked equally well. He thought, *If Clarence comes in from the fields unexpectedly and she isn't there, and he doesn't wonder where she is or go out looking for us* . . . which didn't prevent him from thinking, also, *We can't go on doing this to him. He doesn't deserve it.*

Pulling the bridle over the horse's nose he wondered if they were already the talk of the neighborhood.

"I caught Cletus looking at us."

"What do you mean?"

"As if we'd turned into strangers."

"You imagine it," she said, and kissed him.

He found notes in his pocket that she had put there without his knowing it, and that Marie might have found when she went through his clothes on washday. Were there others that he didn't discover in time?

He waited for his wife to say something and she didn't.

He meant to warn Fern about the notes and forgot.

There was no limit to the falsehood and deception, the smiles he made himself smile, and even so he was caught off guard. Walking from the barn to the house he felt Clarence's arm draped over his shoulder and before he could stop himself he moved away to avoid the physical contact. Also to escape responding to it, which would have been to tell Clarence and get it over with. When it was too late, he wished he had.

7

Innocent (more or less) Creatures

"Lloyd is preoccupied."

It was the first time Cletus had ever heard the word and apparently it didn't mean what you might think.

"About what?" his mother asked.

"I have no idea," his father said.

She didn't for a minute believe him; his manner and his voice and the look in his eyes all betrayed him. He suspected them. Of how much there was no telling. Of something. Another man would have come out with it. As long as he went on pretending not to know, her hands were tied. Maybe that was his game.

She watched him for two days. On the morning of the third, he asked if there was any more coffee and she said accusingly, "You're not fooling me! I know that you know."

When it turned out that she was mistaken and he didn't know, there was no way she could take the words back. It was as if a hole opened suddenly at their feet and they fell into it.

~

Over the mirror in the barbershop there is a colored poster,
framed, of a woman with a pompadour. Her ample bust
emerges from a water lily. She is holding an eyedropper ele-
gantly and advocating Murine for the eyes. On the opposite
wall, a whole row of calendars for the year 1921. On the
linoleum floor, swatches of straight light brown hair. A minute before, they were part of Cletus Smith. Now they are
waiting for the broom. The wall clock says seventeen minutes after two (tick/tock tick/tock) and the odor of bay
rum lingers on the air. Sitting in the barber chair, with
his head pushed down so that his chin is resting on his collar-
bone, Cletus can only look sidewise. He sees a shadow fall
on the plate-glass window and then withdraw abruptly.

With a wave of his clippers the barber indicates the sidewalk, empty now. "Wasn't that your friend?"

The question is not directed at Cletus but at his father,
waiting his turn under the row of calendars. When there is
no answer the barber is not offended. People either answered prying questions, in which case you found out something you didn't know before, or they ignored them and if
you bided your time you found out the answer anyway.
Friend no longer, he remarked to himself. And then his eyebrows rose because of what he saw in the mirror: the boy
was blushing.

Riding on the seat of the cultivator in the field that lay next
to the road, Lloyd Wilson did not raise his head when Clarence drove by in the buckboard wagon, with Cletus on the
seat beside him.

The two men met once, by accident, at the mailboxes,
and after that they saw to it that they didn't meet any-

where. Though they were no longer on speaking terms they couldn't avoid seeing each other at a distance in the fields. And at night the lighted windows of one another's houses, once a comfort, only made them uneasy, since it was a reminder of all the things that were not the way they used to be.

Fred Wilson finished reading the evening paper and took off his glasses in order to rub his eyes. The family resemblance was apparent for a moment. "Well, tomorrow's another day," he said, and stood up.

"Sleep well, Uncle Fred," Marie Wilson said.

"If I don't, I don't know whose fault it will be but mine," he said cheerfully, and went off to his room back of the kitchen. The children said good night to their mother, and then to their father, and went upstairs to bed. The clock ticked, loudly at times. A piece of wood collapsed in the stove. Lloyd Wilson was aware that the silence in the room was not of the ordinary kind, and braced himself. His wife rolled the sock she had just finished darning into a ball and said, "Has something happened between you and Clarence?"

"No."

"You haven't quarreled?"

"No."

"Then what *is* the matter?"

"I don't know."

"You mean you don't know how to tell me?"

He didn't know how to lie. To other people, yes, but not to her. He said slowly, "I guess that's what I do mean." He saw that her face was flushed and her eyes bright with tears. "We—"

"If it's what I think it is, I don't want to hear about it."

"What happened was that we—"

"I told you, I don't want to hear about it."

"—couldn't prevent it."

"And that makes it more comfortable for both of you, I'm sure. But don't ask me to believe it too. From now on you go your way and I'll go mine."

What she meant by this statement he didn't know and it didn't seem like a good time to ask. Their eyes met and with an effort he kept his glance from faltering. The accusing look and the missing front tooth were things he had not bargained for when he stood up before the minister. Or she either, he thought sadly.

Days went by and he had almost come to the conclusion she didn't mean anything by that statement, and that things had settled back into the way they were before, when she announced that she was going to take the children and move in with her sister in town.

He said the first thing that came into his head, which was "But you don't get on with her."

"I know. But she says she'll take us in. Blood being thicker than water."

He sat back and listened while she talked their whole married life out of existence. At no time did he argue with her or deny any statement she made. Finally, when there was nothing more to say, she picked up the lamp and went into the next room, and he followed her, and they undressed and got into bed as if nothing whatever had happened. After a while he said, in the dark, "You can take the girls but not the boys."

There was no answer from the far side of the bed.

He knew that even now he could persuade her to change her mind, but if he did—

"I have never before in my life been happy," he said, "and I will not give it up."

~

Because there wasn't room for everything in the buggy, they took with them only the baby's paraphernalia and what the rest of them needed for the night, and left the battered suitcases and an old leather trunk for him to bring the next day. Nobody spoke all the way in to town. When he pulled on the reins the little girls were ready and one by one jumped from the metal step of the buggy. Hazel stood waiting for her mother to hand the baby down to her. "Be good girls," he called after them but they were too frightened by what was happening to turn and smile at him. He waited until they had all disappeared into the house and then gave the whip a flick. He hadn't meant for things to go this far, and neither had he thought ahead to what might happen next. Coming back to the farm, his spirits lifted for no reason. Or perhaps because a thing hanging over them for so long had at last happened, clearing the air.

Fred never asked questions. The little boys couldn't understand why their mother wasn't there, and he didn't know what she might have said to them, so he told them to be quiet and eat their supper. In the night he heard Orville crying and got up and brought him into his own bed, where he dropped off instantly. But after that he let them cry themselves to sleep, hoping they'd get over it sooner.

He tried to be both mother and father to them, which wasn't easy. When Saturday night came round, he placed the washtub in the middle of the kitchen floor and filled it with warm water from the stove and they stood in it. He poured soapy water over their thin shoulders, as he had seen their mother do, and examined their ears for dirt, but his hands were not as gentle or as practised as hers and Dean looked at him accusingly and said, "You hurt me!"

"Do it yourself, then," he said. But he was damned if he was going to let them grow up in town, not knowing how to handle an axe or plow a straight furrow.

He heard about a widow woman over toward Harmon Springs who was living with relatives and dependent on them for her keep. She might be a little too old for the work but if he got somebody younger, people would talk. "I'll have to think about it," she said when he told her why he had come. She didn't have to think about it very long. As he was getting back into the buggy the front door flew open and she called out to him to wait while she gathered together a few garments. Settling herself on the seat beside him she said, "Just call me 'Mrs. B.'—everybody does." She meant everybody in Harmon Springs.

What with cataracts in both eyes and dizzy spells that came over her if she got down on her knees and poked with the broom in dark corners, the widow didn't do a great deal about the dust that blew into the house from the plowed fields or notice that the pots and pans had acquired a coating of grease. She loved to stand and talk, and one listener was as good as another. "Stop me if I've told you this before, I don't want to repeat myself," she said, but there was no stopping her, or even getting a word in edgewise.

Though she was grateful not to be living on the charity of cousins once removed who raised their eyebrows if she asked for a second helping of chicken and gravy, still the days were long and she wished that people would drop in more. To some she might appear just an ordinary farm woman, but her family had supplied the State of Tennessee with a congressman and a judge. "Well, ma'am, I know you must be right proud of them," Lloyd Wilson said on his way out the door.

It was more than she could do to keep track of his coming and going. Just when she thought he was going to settle

down at last and she could dispose of the things she'd been
saving up to tell him, he put his jacket on and left the house
—to do what, since it was dark outside and the chores were
done, she couldn't imagine.

"Pshaw," she said to the little boys as she went after them
with a washrag. "If you expect to grow up a big strong man
like your father, you can't object to a little soap."

It is not a crime to ask questions, especially indirect ones,
and from Fred Wilson's reluctant answers the widow had
no difficulty in putting two and two together. She also questioned the little boys about their mother, and said primly, "I
hope I shall have the pleasure of meeting her some day."

They did not like her very much but at least she was a
woman, she wore skirts, and so they leaned against her sometimes out of habit or when they missed their mother. They
were very good about coming when she called, and the
rest of the time they wandered around together as if they
were afraid of being separated.

Riding past on his bicycle, Cletus was conscious of the fact
that Mrs. Wilson wasn't there—only that old woman. No
more slices of bread that was still warm from the oven. If
he saw the little boys or Mr. Wilson he stopped to talk to
them. Mr. Wilson acted as though everything was just the
same. "Cletus," he said, "you're looking very spry this morning. Do you think we're in for some more rain?" But it
wasn't the same, if he never came to their house any more
the way he used to. And the Wilson girls weren't going to
be at school to see him graduate from seventh grade.

Wayne had a basket of toys that he kept at Aunt Jenny's
house, but instead of playing with them he followed her

around all morning, talking her leg off—about what she had only a vague idea, for she was only half listening. Finally her patience gave way and she said, "Wayne, honey, be quiet a moment, I can't hear myself think!" And from the way he stood there, looking at her, she realized that he understood perfectly that she was half sick about what was happening out in the country and why his mother was unable to give him her undivided attention, the way she used to. "Not that it matters whether I do or don't hear myself think. You must forgive me, dear heart. I'm not responsible this morning. Now then," and she sat down in a rocking chair and gathered him on her lap and he put his head on her shoulder and they rocked.

After a while he said, "Aunt Jenny, what happens if—what happens if people wake up after they're buried and can't get out?"

"That couldn't happen. They're already in Heaven. And on the Resurrection Day their bodies and their souls are joined and they live happy ever after." Looking at him she could tell that he partly believed what she said and partly didn't believe it, having seen the crows picking at the carcasses of dead animals.

When his mother came to get him he gathered up his things and stood there waiting, but she said, "Run outside and play. Aunt Jenny and I have things to talk about."

The fairgrounds were deserted. The circus had gone ten days before, and it was too soon for the county fair. There was nothing to look at and nobody to talk to. When he got tired of waiting on the front steps he went back into the house and his mother made him go outdoors again.

It will wear itself out, Clarence said to himself, provided he was patient and didn't drive Fern to do something foolish.

He was patient, up to a point. For him, he was very patient. But she knew just where he drew the line, and, daring him, stepped over it. When he lost his temper he did things he could hardly believe afterward. Once when they were having an argument she screamed and Victor picked up a bucket of water and threw it over him. The shock brought him to his senses. He looked down and saw he had the poker in his hand.

What *she* did she did deliberately, and she never said she was sorry.

Somebody turned the wick of the lamp up too high and it made a fine layer of soot over everything. He expected her to burst into tears and start taking down the front-room curtains. Instead she laughed.

He asked her to go with him to see his parents and she refused. "But if you don't come they'll think we aren't getting along."

"Which is only the truth."

"They've had enough trouble in their lives. I don't want to add to it."

"You won't be," she said. "They know. Everybody knows. That's all people have to think about."

Since there was work to be done outside, he gave up and reached for his jacket.

All his socks had holes in them. The strawberry bed was loaded with fruit and she didn't bother to pick it. She left the beans on the vines until they were too big to eat. He no longer had a wife—only a prisoner.

Unwatered too long, the Christmas cactus in the front window died and ended up on the rubbish pile. When it was time for her plate of scraps the dog came and wolfed them down and then withdrew into her house. The cats followed Fern Smith around, purring as usual, and with their tails straight up in the air. Since they were neither faithful nor obedient themselves they saw no reason why women should be.

The widow knew that if she talked long enough at Fred Wilson he would have to lower the newspaper that hid his face and listen to her. Whether he wanted to or not. He heard about the habits of her late husband, and the hard life they had had—so much sickness, and losing the farm because they couldn't keep up payments on the mortgage, the younger son, her favorite, dead of a ruptured appendix, the older one who seldom came to see her because his wife made trouble if he did, and the daughter who lived too far away and never wrote except once in a great while, to say that things were not going well with them. In exchange for all this information which he did not particularly want, Fred Wilson felt obliged to tell her something, so he told her about his wife's lingering illness. "Poor thing," she said sympathetically. "But she's better off now. She's out of it at last."

When he said how grateful he was to his nephew for taking him in after she died, the widow said, "But wouldn't you be happier in your own home?"

"I loved my wife too much ever to remarry," he said firmly. He might not be able to read everybody's mind but he had no trouble reading hers.

The widow had other strings to her bow. One day she met Colonel Dowling in the Smiths' lane and he bowed to her and she never got over it. The social life that went on in her mind was vivid and kept her from being lonely. When Colonel Dowling said *Mrs. B., would you care to take a spin in my car?* she said *No, thank you,* or *Well, since you insist,* depending on her mood.

~

At Aunt Jenny's house, in a dresser drawer crammed with odds and ends of female clutter, there is an oval picture of her at the age of twenty-three. Every other picture of herself she has destroyed. She was never a beautiful woman but neither was she as plain as she imagined. When this picture was taken she was head over heels in love with Tom Evans, but for some reason love, even of the most ardent and soul-destroying kind, is never caught by the lens of the camera. One would almost think it didn't exist.

Downstairs, on a bracket shelf next to a vase with hand-painted pink roses on it, there is a matching picture of him, taken at the same time. His hair is roached and he is wearing a high stiff collar, and hardly anything shows in his face but his Welsh ancestry. His father and mother were rabid Methodists, but the rigid attitudes that they tried to hand down to him did not stand the test of experience and he ended up not believing in God. "I believe in paying your bills on time," he said, when he wanted to excite the pious. "And in common politeness."

He worked hard, because he liked to work, and was thrifty because he enjoyed that also. He worked for somebody else not because he had an ordinary mind but because the town wouldn't support a second plumbing business. Occasionally he treated himself to a glass of beer but the swinging doors of a saloon did not have an irresistible attraction for him. His fastidiousness could be explained easily enough by assuming that a nobleman's child and a commoner's had been switched in their cradles. But in Logan County there are no castles for the baby to be carried from in the middle of the night, and in fact no noblemen. So there must have been some other explanation.

He died in agony, of a gall-bladder attack, when he was in his early fifties, and the oval photograph, adapting itself to circumstances, is now clearly the photograph of a dead man.

He could not have loved Fern more if she had been his own daughter. To an outsider it seemed that Aunt Jenny was relegated to the position of waiting on them. Waiting on them was her whole pleasure, and she did not ask herself whether they valued her sufficiently. Or at all. Innocence is defined in dictionaries as freedom from guilt or sin, especially through lack of knowledge; purity of heart; blamelessness; guilelessness; artlessness; simplicity, etc. There is no aspect of the word that does not apply to her.

Without the heavyset aristocratic man snoring away on his side of the bed, without the fresh-eyed child whose hair ribbon needs retying; without the conversation at meals and the hearty appetites and getting dressed for church on time; without the tears of laughter and the worry about making both ends meet, the unpaid bills, the layoffs, both seasonal and unexpected; without the toys that have to be picked up lest somebody trip over them, and the seven shirts that have to be washed and ironed, one for every day in the week; without the scraped knee and the hurt feelings, the misunderstandings that need to be cleared up, the voices calling for her so that she is perpetually having to stop what she is doing and go see what they want—without all this, what have you? A mystery: How is it that she didn't realize it was going to last such a short time?

When Lloyd Wilson got upset at the thought of the money that used to be in his savings account in the Lincoln National Bank and wasn't there any longer, he reminded himself that he had a chance to object to the amount of the settlement and just said, "Where do I sign?" She had cleaned him out, but he owed her something, and he couldn't let his children starve. It didn't occur to him, though, that she would turn the little girls against him. They sat with their mother in church, all in a row, and if he tried to catch their eye or smiled at them they looked straight ahead at nothing.

When they were older they would feel different, maybe, but all the same, it hurt his feelings. He changed his life insurance policies so that the boys were the sole beneficiaries.

Mrs. Stroud drove out to her farm earlier in the day to avoid the heat. While they were inspecting the corncribs she said crossly, "Your marital difficulties do not interest me but I don't like to see this place going to wrack and ruin because of them. The woman you have hired to keep house for you is old and half blind, and the house is by no means the way your wife kept it."

"I know," he said, for once neither evasive nor verging on insolence.

"My house in town is always clean and I see no reason why this house, which, after all, is mine too, shouldn't be the same way."

"I'll speak to her," he said soberly, but he didn't. As though he were gifted with second sight, he regarded the arrangement as temporary.

As Cletus walked into the cool shade of the house he heard voices. His mother's voice. And then Aunt Jenny's. He knew the cookie jar was empty but he put his hand in it anyway, hoping to be surprised, and as he felt around inside, his mother said, "That was last Saturday. Naturally I was nervous but it turned out there was no cause to be." She waited until he had gone upstairs to his room before she continued: "When I got home I said to you know who, I said, 'It may interest you to know that I've consulted a lawyer.' I decided the time had come to tell him."

"I don't know as I'd have done that," Aunt Jenny said. "That is, not if you're meaning to avoid trouble."

Fern Smith wasn't meaning to avoid trouble; she was bent on making it. It was her only hope.

"It set him back on his heels. I knew it would."

Aunt Jenny raised her eyes to indicate the ventilator in the ceiling.

"If we don't mention any names, how can Cletus tell who we're talking about? And I haven't mentioned any."

"What did he say?"

"Clarence?"

"No, the man in town."

"He listened, and asked questions, and finally he said, 'Mrs. Smith, I think we can safely say we have a case.' "

A case of what, Cletus wondered.

With Lloyd Wilson's wife gone, what prevented her from throwing a shawl over her shoulders and running across the fields to his house? The whole community. It was one thing to behave in such a way as to provoke gossip and quite another for them to live in open immorality. They had talked about it often. She didn't care if every woman she knew stopped speaking to her, but they wouldn't let their husbands have anything to do with him, and that might make it very difficult. There wasn't a man for miles around who wasn't indebted to him for something, but the only one who ever seemed to feel this was Clarence.

And Mrs. Stroud?

He didn't know. With her, anything was possible. When she came out to the farm these days she had a cat-and-mouse expression on her face that was new—as if she was enjoying the situation he had got himself into and was watching with amusement to see what he would do next.

People will stand only so much. And there is a line that you can't cross over, no matter how much you would like to. If he did cross over it and he got a letter informing him that after the first of March Mrs. Stroud had no further need for his services, where would they go then? Who would take him on as a tenant when they found out that he was living with a woman who was not his wife? Their courage failed them.

Clarence believed Fern when she said that she had neither seen Lloyd nor talked to him, but he knew in his bones that they communicated with each other somehow. He questioned the boys and searched in odd corners about the farm —a hollow tree, an abandoned chicken house, a shed that was far enough from the house so that Lloyd could have gone there at night without the risk of being seen. But the dog would have barked, and the boys clearly knew nothing. About that, anyway. How much else they knew he didn't like to think. One minute she was careful and talked in a low voice, or she would get up and shut the door. And then suddenly it didn't matter to her any more what she said or who heard her. Standing at the head of the stairs in her nightgown, she shouted down at him, "You treat the horses better than you treat me!" It wasn't true, and she knew it.

She said she had been in love with somebody else when she married him. He didn't know whether to believe her or not; it might be something she made up on the spur of the moment, to knock the wind out of him.

He drove in to town and got drunk and came home and

climbed on top of her. It didn't work. She fought like a wild-cat, and he fell off the bed and lay tangled up in the bed-clothes. In a sudden weariness of soul he dropped off to sleep and woke in broad daylight, with a hangover and a foul taste in his mouth. The bed was empty.

He went to see the Baptist minister and they had a long talk. In the minister's study, with the door closed. Some things he could hardly bring himself to say, but he felt bet-ter after he had said them. And the expression on the minis-ter's face was sympathetic when he said, "Why don't we kneel down right now and ask for God's help." So they did. And he wasn't embarrassed. At that point he would have done anything.

Standing by the front door, with the rain blowing in their faces, the minister said, "Tell her to come and see me. It may be that I can show her where the path of duty lies."

Fern Smith didn't go to see him. Instead she went to town, to the little house across from the fairgrounds. When Aunt Jenny's opinion didn't conform to hers it could be brushed aside.

The widow could not let a farm wagon pass by without running to the front window to see who was *in* the wagon. It wasn't likely, therefore, that she would fail to notice that her employer had something on his mind. Poor man, he missed his family and was regretting the way he had be-haved. She intended to try and make him understand—she was just waiting for the auspicious moment—that he mustn't be afraid his wife wouldn't forgive him. If he went to her in the right spirit and told her how sorry he was, things were bound to work out the way he wanted them to. And when his wife did forgive him and came home, then she might be glad of a little help with the housework.

And if not? . . .

Bravely, Mrs. B. decided she was not going to let selfish considerations stand in the way of Lloyd's happiness.

When Cletus walked into the cow barn the cats ran to greet him. His father was already there, milking Flossie. Victor should have been milking the cow on the other side of him but he had gone off on a bender, even though it wasn't a national holiday. Cletus picked up a milk bucket and stool and sat down. He tried to adjust the rhythm of his squirt-squirt to his father's. Old Bess moved her feet restlessly and he said, "So, boss." The cats rubbed against his ankles, purring, but he didn't feel them. The night before, the terrible voice had given him something new to worry about: *I can walk out of this house any time I feel like it, taking the boys with me.* He fell back into the same deep sleep as if nothing had happened, but this morning, while he was mooning over his cereal, there it was.

He saw that Blackie was sitting with his pink mouth stretched wide open and he squirted a stream of milk into it. Sixteen years old that cat was, and his ears all cut up from fighting, and hardly a tooth in his head.

She won't do it, Cletus thought. But why shouldn't she? What was there to stop her, except fear of his father, and she wasn't afraid, of anything or anybody.

The level of milk rose in the two pails. His father whistled the same sad tune he whistled all day long. When he stood up, Cletus said, "Last night I heard something."

"Outside?"

"No."

"Shouldn't listen to conversations that don't concern you."

"I wasn't trying to listen."

"I see. Well, what did you hear?"

"Mama said, *she* said she might move into town and take me and Wayne with her."

"We'll cross that bridge when we come to it."

"Pa . . ."

"Yes, son."

"Promise me you won't get sore if I say something?" He waited and there was no answer from the next stall. "Please don't argue with her about it, Pa."

"Why not? Do you want to move into town with her?"

"You know I don't. But you shouldn't have said you wouldn't let her do it. If you tell her she can't do something, then she has to do it."

"Why, you little fucker!"

The heavy hand shot out and sent him sprawling. What the boy had said was true, but a lot of difference that made. The bucket was overturned, a pool of milk began to spread along the barn floor. With his right ear roaring with pain and one whole side of his face gone numb, he picked himself up and drew the stool out from between the cow's legs and put the bucket under her. He managed not to cry, but his hands shook, and the milk squirted unevenly into the pail.

"The next time you try to tell me how to run my affairs it won't be just a clout on the head, I'll break your God damn back," Clarence Smith said. He picked up his stool and moved on to the adjoining stall and sat down and, with his head pressed against the cow's side, resumed his sad whistling.

The conversation didn't turn out the way the widow expected. She thought Lloyd Wilson would open his heart to her and instead he said, "Yes, well, I'll think about it," and picked up the *Farmer's Almanac*.

She paused in her crocheting and pushed the lamp closer to him. Either he didn't want to talk about it or he had something else on his mind that he couldn't bring himself to discuss with her. Maybe money troubles. Or it could be that Mrs. Stroud was making difficulty. She was not a very nice woman and had her nose into everything.

8

The Machinery of Justice

Clarence was fastening the pasture gate with a loop of wire when it came over him that she was gone. He broke into a run. In his mind he saw the note propped against the sugar bowl on the kitchen table. When he flung the door open she was standing at the stove, her hair damp with steam, stirring the clothes in the big copper boiler. They stared at each other a moment and then she said, "No, I'm still here."

When she did leave, six weeks later, he had no premonition of it.

He was informed, through the mail, by her lawyer, that any attempt to get in touch with her or with their children except through him could be considered as constituting harassment, and that whatever steps were necessary to protect her from it would be taken.

The next thing that happened was a notice from the county clerk's office: she was suing him for a divorce.

Shortly thereafter, Fern Smith sat in her lawyer's office discussing a notice she had received from Clarence's lawyer. It was out of their hands now. They had stopped shouting at each other and put their faith in legal counsel. With the result that how things could be made to look was what counted, not how they actually were.

The divorce proceedings and the cross bill were tried as a

single case in the fall term of court. In the jury box and in the visitors' part of the courtroom were men Clarence Smith knew, and, averting his eyes from them, he had to sit and hear his most intimate life laid bare. He did not recognize the description of himself, and he wondered how Fern's lawyer could utter with such a ring of sincerity statements he must know had no foundation in truth. Or how she could sit there looking like a victim when it was she who had made it all come about. Her lawyer had found half a dozen witnesses who were pleased to testify to his bad temper—which surprised him. He had not known that he had any enemies. He had only one witness for his side, but he was counting on that one witness to establish the falsehood of everything that was said.

All but unrecognizable in a new suit and shaved by the barber, the hired man testified to "intimacies." He used other words that had been put in his mouth by Clarence's lawyer. On various occasions, he said, he had come upon the plaintiff and Wilson in an embrace or kissing, or with his hand inside her blouse. When his employer was off the property, Wilson would come to the house and the shade in the upstairs bedroom would be drawn and it would be an hour or more sometimes before he reappeared.

Pacing back and forth in front of the jury box, Fern Smith's lawyer spoke eloquently of the close ties that bound the two households together, and in particular of the friendship of the two men. Was it not a fact, was it not an incontrovertible fact that over a period of many years before the present discord arose, and with Clarence Smith's full knowledge and approval, Lloyd Wilson had frequently gone to the Smiths' house when Smith was off the premises? Before proceeding with the cross-examination, he would like to offer, as evidence bearing on the reliability of the witness's testimony, the fact that he was seldom without the smell of liquor on his breath, and that he had spent the night of July 4th in jail in an inebriated condition.

Clarence's lawyer leapt to his feet and exclaimed, "Your Honor, I object," and the judge said sourly, "Objection overruled."

Victor was easily trapped into saying things he did not mean, and that could not be true, and his confusion was such that the courtroom was moved to laughter again and again. After that, Clarence was called to the witness stand and placed under oath, and heard acts of his described that he could not truthfully deny. What Fern's lawyer did not tell the gentlemen of the jury was the provocation that led up to this violent behavior. And when Clarence tried to, he was instructed by the judge to confine his remarks to answering the questions put to him by counsel.

Nobody said, in court, that Clarence Smith was pierced to the heart by his wife's failure to love him, and it wouldn't have made any difference if they had.

The evening paper reported that Mrs. Fern Smith was granted a decree of divorce against her husband, on the grounds of extreme and repeated cruelty, the charges in his cross bill not being substantiated in the eyes of the jury. He was ordered to pay fifty dollars a month alimony, and she was granted custody of the children.

The ringing of the locusts wore itself out and stopped, only to start up again in the treetops. With Aunt Jenny standing over him telling him what to do next, Cletus carried load after load of junk up the outside cellar stairs and on out to the alley. Cans of long-dried paint and varnish. Jars of preserve that had gone bad or were too old to be trusted. Empty medicine bottles. Bundles of old magazines and newspapers. An iron bedstead. A chair with a cane seat that had given way. A sheet-iron stove with one leg missing. A ten-gallon milk can with a hole in the bottom. Screens so eaten with rust that you could put your finger through them. Occasionally she would decide that something—a bamboo picture frame with its glass broken or a silk dress that was stained under the arms—was too good to throw away, and it was put aside until she could recollect somebody who would be glad to have it. Going through a box of old letters, she came upon a canceled bankbook and turned the pages thoughtfully. "I have a little money," she remarked. (*Why did she say that? It was the one thing she meant to tell nobody. . . .*) "Tom had a life insurance policy that was all paid up when he died. I may not be in the same class with John D. Rockefeller, but you'd find that five thousand dollars was a lot of money if you tried to save it. . . . It'll go to your mother when I die. I just wanted you to know how things are." Which wasn't exactly the truth; what she really wanted was for him to say something—to be surprised by this cat she had inadvertently let out of the bag. "I mean you won't starve," she said.

It took both of them to carry the horsehair mattress spotted with mildew. As they were coming back from the alley, she said, "That's enough for today. There's a store-room that needs cleaning out but it can wait." He closed the cellar door, she gave him the padlock, which had been in her apron pocket, and they went into the house by way of the back porch. She wanted to say *I don't like the way things have turned out any better than you do*, and was afraid to say it lest Cletus think she wasn't glad to have them under her roof.

She made him wash his hands at the kitchen sink and gave him a glass of cold milk and a large piece of gooseberry pie.

Leaning against the sink, he took a swallow of milk and

then said, "When Victor and Pa come in from the fields, who
gets their meals?"

"Nobody, so far as I know. It isn't easy for them, I'm
sure, but any man knows how to fry bacon and eggs and
make coffee."

"They're used to eating more than that."

"He may have to get somebody to keep house for him,
like Mr. Wilson," she said, and could have bit her tongue
out.

"You'll have Sunday dinner with us, won't you?" his mother
said. "Come right from church, so we can have a good
visit."

There was no way Clarence could say no or he would
have. He didn't tell her that he had stopped going to church.

When they sat down to the table, he saw that his mother
had cooked all his favorite dishes, and he tried to eat, though
he had no appetite. From his father's uneasiness and from
the careful absence of any expression on her face, he knew
that her feelings were hurt. She had expected him to tell
them everything he couldn't tell the judge and the jury, and
when he didn't she thought it was because he didn't trust
them.

"We've been expecting the boys to pay us a visit," she said,
"but so far they haven't. I dare say Fern won't allow it."

"I don't imagine she would do that," he said, avoiding her
glance.

His mother and father were the only two people on earth
he trusted at this point, but where to begin? With the fact
that he was having trouble scraping together the money to
pay his ex-wife's alimony? There wasn't anything he could
tell them that wouldn't make them grieve, and anyway, he
couldn't bear to talk about it.

He knew what had been done to him but not what he had done to deserve it.

It would have been a help if at some time some Baptist preacher, resting his forearms on the pulpit and hunching his shoulders, had said *People neither get what they deserve nor deserve what they get. The gentle and the trusting are trampled on. The rich man usually forces his way through the eye of the needle, and there is little or no point in putting your faith in Divine Providence.* . . . On the other hand, how could any preacher, Baptist or otherwise, say this?

Fern was advised by her attorney that it would be better if she and Lloyd Wilson didn't see each other for a time. When they wrote to each other, they were careful to post the letters themselves. Her letters were very long, his short. It was not natural to him to put his feelings on paper. But as she read and reread his letters, the words that were not there were put there by her imagination, until she was satisfied that he really did love her as much as she loved him.

The dog waited every afternoon by the mailbox. She knew when it was time to round up the cows, but the boy might come and not find her there. So she went on waiting, and when she saw the man coming toward her she ran off into a cornfield, but only a little ways. She didn't really try to escape the beating she knew he was going to give her.

Cletus started to ride out to the farm on his bicycle and his mother said, "Where are you going?" and he told her and she said, "I'd rather you didn't." When he asked why not, she looked unhappy and said, "Please don't argue with me,

Cletus. If your father wants to see you, he'll say so."

It was only a hairline hesitation that kept her from telling him everything. Eventually, when he was grown, she would sit down with him some day and tell him the whole story from the beginning, and he would appreciate all she had been through, and forgive her. *Your father wouldn't give me my freedom,* she would say, *and so I had to go to court and get it that way. . . .* In these imaginary conversations it did not occur to her that he might not forgive her. *If Lloyd hadn't been in love with me,* she imagined herself saying. *Or if he had loved his wife, I guess I would have gone on being married to your father, ill-suited to each other though we were. . . .*

At the memory of Lloyd Wilson's hands resting on her shoulders as he bent down and kissed her, she shuddered with happiness.

By staring at her fixedly, Wayne made the acquaintance of a little girl named Patsy, who lived four or five houses down the street from Aunt Jenny's house. She had a tricycle, which they rode up and down the cement sidewalk, and only now and then did they quarrel about whose turn it was. He went to Patsy's house early in the morning, and when lunchtime came and Patsy's mother asked him if he would like to stay and eat with them, he always said yes. When she said, "Don't you think it would be a good idea if you ran home and told your mother?" he said, "She won't mind."

Patsy's mother thought it would be nice if Wayne's mother said, "Thank you for being so nice to my little boy," or something of that kind, instead of not even bothering to look up when she was passing the house. And her name in the paper and all.

~

In a town the size of Lincoln there are no well-kept secrets. Somebody told somebody who told somebody who told somebody who told Clarence about the fat letters with no return address that Fern dropped in the big green box in front of the post office after dark. It didn't even take very long for this to happen. Or for Fern to find out that Clarence knew.

Only now, after the long battle had been won, did she become frightened. She found herself thinking, for the first time, about Clarence. About what she had done to him. And what he might be capable of. She hadn't wanted to take the fifty dollars a month alimony. It was the lawyer's idea. She found herself reliving the moment when Clarence picked up the poker and started for her. And other moments like it.

The dog came racing down the lane and threw herself upon Cletus, and he let the bicycle fall and buried his face in her fur. But after that, nothing was the way he thought it would be. He had expected to follow his father around, helping him with whatever he was doing, and instead they sat in the house all afternoon, trying to think of things to say.

"Thou shalt not bear false witness," the Bible said—but why not, if the jury couldn't tell the difference between the truth and a pack of lies and neither could the judge? Dressed in black and wearing a veil as if she was in mourning for him, dabbing her eyes with her handkerchief, she fooled them all. The Bible also said, "Thou shalt not covet thy neighbor's wife," and he was ordered to pay them fifty dollars a month. That was their reward, for breaking the Ten Commandments.

How was he to explain this to a half-grown boy? Also he

was ashamed—ashamed and embarrassed at all his son had been put through. He knew that Cletus would have preferred to stay out here with him and he couldn't even manage that.

As a result of that humiliating day in court Clarence Smith's sense of cause and effect suffered a permanent distortion. His mind was filled with thoughts that, taken one by one, were perfectly reasonable but in sequence did not quite make sense.

He had no idea how long some of his silences were.

At last the hands of the clock allowed him to say, "It's time you were starting back to town."

"Can't I stay and help with the milking?"

"You don't want to be on the road on a bicycle after dark."

"I could get out of the way if a car comes."

"You better go now. Your mother will worry about you."

He waved goodbye to his father, who was standing on the porch steps, and kicked the standard of his bicycle up into the catch on the rear mudguard and said, "No, Trixie. Don't look at me like that. You can't go with me. . . . No . . . No, do you hear? *No!*"

On the following Saturday he asked his mother if he could ride out to the farm and again she said, "I'd rather you didn't."

She couldn't bear to tell him that his father had sent word by a neighbor that she was not to let him come any more.

Whether they are part of home or home is part of them is not a question children are prepared to answer. Having taken away the dog, take away the kitchen—the smell of something good in the oven for dinner. Also the smell of washday, of wool drying on the wooden rack. Of ashes. Of soup simmering on the stove. Take away the patient old horse waiting by the pasture fence. Take away the chores that kept him busy from the time he got home from school until they sat down to supper. Take away the early-morning mist, the sound of crows quarreling in the treetops.

His work clothes are still hanging on a nail beside the door of his room, but nobody puts them on or takes them off. Nobody sleeps in his bed. Or reads the broken-backed copy of *Tom Swift and His Flying Machine*. Take that away too, while you are at it.

Take away the pitcher and bowl, both of them dry and dusty. Take away the cow barn where the cats, sitting all in a row, wait with their mouths wide open for somebody to squirt milk down their throats. Take away the horse barn too—the smell of hay and dust and horse piss and old sweat-stained leather, and the rain beating down on the plowed field beyond the open door. Take all this away and what have you done to him? In the face of a deprivation so great, what is the use of asking him to go on being the boy he was. He might as well start life over again as some other boy instead.

Just when she had about given up hoping, the widow met Lloyd Wilson's wife and was much taken with her.

Fingering a list of things that only she knew where to put her hands on, in chests and dresser drawers and cardboard boxes pushed back under the eaves in the attic, Marie Wilson made polite conversation. She could hardly believe the disorder and filth that met her eyes everywhere she looked. The windows were so thickly coated with dust and cobwebs you could hardly see out of them. The table runner on the parlor table had ink stains on it, and somebody had burned a hole in the big rag rug that it had taken her all one winter to make. She knew without having to look that no broom ever went searching for lint under the beds. The place hadn't been aired for weeks, and the whole house but especially the downstairs bedroom stank of kerosene and sweaty clothing and stale human breath. Clapping her hands together she caught a clothes moth.

What the widow was waiting for as she talked on and on was a sign that the approval was reciprocated. Sitting on the edge of her chair, Marie Wilson said, "That's quite true," and "I know what you mean," and "I'm sure you're right," and finally, reaching the end of her patience, she said, "I'm afraid you'll have to excuse me, I have things to do." Still talking, the widow followed her up the attic stairs.

But it was the little boys that upset her most. They were thin and pale and answered her questions listlessly, as if they were addressing a stranger. She said, "You know that your father wouldn't let me take you with me?" and they nodded. She brushed the hair out of their eyes, and kissed them, and touched them on the cheek and on the shoulder as she talked to them, and the strangeness wore off eventually. After that they wouldn't let her out of their sight. As she bent down to say goodbye to them they both started to cry.

Lloyd had driven in to town to get her and when she had gathered up what she wanted he drove her back. She did not criticize the widow's housekeeping. It was his business who he got to look after him. They had sat in an uncomfortable silence all the way out to the farm, but now he began to talk about the possibility of his finding a place somewhere in Iowa—which would mean that she would never see the boys at all. She asked him to bring them in to town now and then to spend the night with her and he answered, "It would

only make it worse for them." After which they both re-
lapsed into silence. He could feel that there was something on
the tip of her tongue which for some reason she kept decid-
ing not to say. When he stopped in front of the boarding
house where she was now living she started to get out of the
buggy and then turned to him and said, "I know you don't
care in the least about me, or your daughters, but I don't
see how you could do that to Clarence."

He looked down at his hands, with the reins looped
through his fingers, and didn't answer.

It rained and rained, and when the sky cleared there was a
light frost. The leaves started falling, and the dog could see
stars shining in the tops of the trees. Having run away and
been whipped for it until she could hardly stand, she stayed
on the property. If she went looking for the boy it was never
farther than the foot of the lane. Sometimes Clarence forgot
to feed her and she had to remind him. What he put in her
pan was not at all like the scraps the woman used to give
her.

The lawyer who had presented Clarence's case in court so
badly sent him a much larger bill than he had expected.
Though there was plenty of work that needed doing outside,
he sat in the house brooding. The dog came and stood looking in at him through the screen door, and he burst out at
her in a rage and she crept away.

Lloyd Wilson went to see his wife and asked her once more
to divorce him so that he and Fern could marry. She listened
to what he had to say and then replied that she would think
about it. From her tone of voice he knew what her answer

would be. She was not going to divorce him, and he had no grounds for divorcing her.

Her eyelids were closed but Fern wasn't asleep. She knew that she slept sometimes, because she passed in and out of dreaming. Daybreak was a comfort. The birds. A rooster crowing. It meant that time existed. At night everything stood still.

The milkman, clinking his bottles. People went about their rounds, things happened that had nothing to do with her divorce—this she needed to be reminded of. It would have been a further comfort to get up and go downstairs and make a pot of coffee, but then she would wake Aunt Jenny in the front room. Sometimes she dozed. When she let go completely it was always with a jerk that shook the bed and brought her wide awake.

As if she were watching a play she relived the time Tom locked her in her room. How old was she? Eighteen? Nineteen? "You're too young to know your own mind," he said. On the other hand she wasn't too young to have fallen in love with a man with a wife and two children. "I won't have you breaking up somebody's home!" he shouted. And she said—even as the words came out of her mouth she regretted them—she said, "You're not my father and I won't have you or anybody else telling me what I can or can't do." So he locked her in her room, and she climbed out the window onto the roof of the back porch and slid down the drainpipe. He knew what was happening but didn't stir from his chair. When she got home, he was still sitting there and they had it out, at two o'clock in the morning.

Whether she would have accepted Clarence if she hadn't been sick with love for a man she couldn't have was a question she had never until now tried to answer. At all events, when Clarence turned up and began courting her there wasn't any shouting. Tom was polite to him but distant. And he said nothing whatever to her. He didn't need to. She knew that he prided himself on his ability to maneuver people around to the position he wanted them to take and usually he was successful, but not this time. Not with her. She came to the table with her face set, and the two of them ate in silence, unless Aunt Jenny said something, and even then they didn't always bother to answer. When she burst out, "What is it you have against him?" he wiped his mouth with his napkin and leaned back in his chair and looked at her. Then he said "Are you sure you want to hear it?" and she said "Yes."

Perhaps at another time in her life she might have listened to him and have considered the fact that nobody had ever understood her the way he did. But in the reckless mood she was in, it was his very understanding that drove her to act. She had to prove to him that he could be wrong too; that things were not necessarily always the way he thought.

At one point she interrupted him and he said, "Just let me finish. When you are picking a husband there are only two things that count—good blood and a good disposition. One day, on the courthouse square, before ever he turned up here, I saw him taking something out on his horses. I didn't enjoy it. And you wouldn't have, either." He sat looking at her for a moment and then he said, "I see I might as well have been addressing a fence post. Try to understand that other people are real and have feelings too. And some things, once they are done, can't be undone." And he got up and left the table.

When she announced that she and Clarence were going to be married and live on a farm in McLean County he said, "Very well, but don't expect me to give you my blessing or come to the wedding."

~

The wild geese were flying south.

The nights turned cold. They finished shucking the corn. And one day Victor and Clarence came out of the house and stood together talking. Victor was wearing the new suit, and he had an old leather satchel with him. Since Clarence had been cleaned out by the lawsuit and couldn't afford to pay him anything, he had offered to work for his keep. The offer was not accepted.

"I hope everything goes all right with you," he said now, shading his eyes from the direct light of the sun.

"I'll manage somehow, I guess," Clarence said, and they shook hands.

"You can always reach me through my sister in New Holland."

Victor picked up the satchel and started off down the lane, and that was the last the dog ever saw of him.

It turned warm again and there was a week of fine weather. Except for the oak trees, all the leaves had fallen. Otherwise it was like summer. With her paws resting on her nose, the dog followed the circling of a big horsefly, and when it zoomed off she closed her eyes and went to sleep, and dreamed that she was chasing a rabbit.

Instead of getting on a train and going to Iowa to look for good land, Lloyd Wilson temporized. He told himself he couldn't leave before the first of November, and then it was November and the days went by and there was always something that needed doing, and with one excuse and another he kept himself from facing the fact that what he was proposing to do was impossible. He had spent his whole life on this place and leave it he could not. Even though the

things people were saying about Clarence made it sound
like he was more than half crazy and capable of anything.

"You haven't given me much notice," Colonel Dowling
said. "And I don't know that I can find somebody over-
night."

He noticed that Clarence put his finger inside his collar,
as if it were choking him, and that his hands were restless,
and he stuttered. None of this was at all like him. But he was
prepared to give his tenant a satisfactory character, as far as
it went. An unqualified recommendation wouldn't have been
right, in the circumstances. He just wasn't the man he used
to be, before he dragged his wife into court and all that.
But it ought to be possible to say something sufficiently
commendatory so that Clarence could still manage to find a
place. The praise shouldn't be of so specific a kind that, if
there was trouble later on, the people that took him on as
their tenant would feel that he, the Colonel, had been less
than candid. One way or another, he would work it out.
He was at his best with ambiguities of this kind.

To his surprise, Clarence didn't ask for any recommendation. Instead he shook hands and walked down the rickety
wooden stairs and out onto the sidewalk, where he stood
blinking in the harsh sunlight. He now had no wife, no family, and no farm, all through Lloyd Wilson's doing.

It snowed and then there were three or four days of soft
weather, leaving the ground bare again. After that, the
nights were very cold.

It was the time of year when the man usually sawed up
fallen trees and split the logs and filled the woodshed with
firewood. The dog took note of the fact that he didn't do

any of these things. The woods were alive with quail and pheasant and he didn't go hunting.

The new tenant turned up with an acquaintance, a bald-headed older man whom he kept turning to for his opinion. They went through the house with Clarence, and then they walked around outside, inspecting the barns and the outbuildings, and asking a great many questions about yield and acreage. At one point all three men turned to look at the dog, and it didn't take any great intelligence on her part to know who it was they were discussing.

Cletus didn't feel like hanging around the schoolyard after school, watching boys he didn't know (and who showed no signs of wanting to know him) shoot baskets. So he came straight home, if you could call it that, even though there was nothing to do when he got there. He opened the door of the icebox and a female voice called from the front room, "Cletus, you'll spoil your supper," so he closed the door again—there wasn't anything he wanted anyway—and went outdoors and sat on the back steps, in the bleak sunshine.

The teacher, who was not young or pretty, had given each of them a map of South America and told them to fill in the names of the countries and rivers, but Cletus didn't feel like it. With a stick he drew crosses in the dirt, making life difficult for an ant who had business in that patch of bare ground. Though it had been going on for days, he was only now aware of a distant hammering: *Pung, pung, pung, ka-pung, kapung, kapung, kapung* . . . Somebody must be building a new house.

Twisting the heel of his shoe he erased the lines he had drawn in the dirt and, with them, the ant. Then he got up and went toward the hole in the back fence.

When the man and the old man started bringing things out of the house, the dog couldn't imagine what had got into them. Bedsteads, mattresses, chairs. Tables, kitchen utensils, tools. Boxes of this and that. All out on the grass where they would get rained on.

The old man said, "Are you sure you want to get rid of this nice set of encyclopedia?"

"If you want it, put it in the car, Dad," Clarence said.

The farmyard began to fill up with people and he shut her up in the woodshed, though she wasn't meaning to do anything unless called upon. All she could see was the light that came through the cracks between the boards, but she could hear perfectly. More and more buggies and wagons kept arriving, and a person with a very loud voice kept shouting, "Wullabulla, wullabulla," and pounding on a table with a wooden mallet in such a way that it hurt her ears, *and the animals seemed to be leaving!* First the cows, that she had the privilege of rounding up every evening of her life. And then the sheep. She could hear them baaing with fright. Then the hogs. Then the chickens and turkeys. And finally the horses, which was too much. How was the man going to plow without them? It must be the work of the loud voice, and if the man had only opened the door of the woodshed the dog would have helped him drive that person clean off the property. To remind him that she was there, able and willing, she barked and barked.

When he finally did let her out, the shouting had stopped and all the things that had been standing about on the grass were either gone or in somebody's buggy or wagon, and the few people who were left were going, and the sun was already down behind the hill.

Clarence got a length of rope and tied the dog to a tree, which she didn't understand any more than she understood why he felt it was necessary to shut her up in the shed. Then he brought some more things out of the house—a suitcase, fishing poles, a flashlight, an axe, an umbrella—and put them in the car. The old man pointed to the doghouse, and Clarence said, "That stays here."

While his father waited in the car, Clarence walked through all the empty rooms one last time. Then he locked the kitchen door and put the key under the mat. "I'm glad this day is over," he said and, taking a firm stance in front of the car radiator, he gave the crank half a dozen quick heaves and then ran around and climbed into the driver's seat. The roar of the engine diminished as he adjusted the spark.

The old man saw the dog looking at them expectantly and said, "What if that fella doesn't come?"

"He'll come," Clarence said. "He told me it might be dark before he got here, but he promised me he'd come today."

The borrowed Model T drove off down the lane and the dog was tied up, with night coming on, and no lights in the house, and no smoke going up the chimney.

She waited a long long time, trying not to worry. Trying to be good—trying to be especially good. And telling herself that they had only gone in to town and were coming right back, even though it was perfectly obvious that this wasn't true. Not the way they acted. Eventually, in spite of her, the howls broke out. Sitting on her haunches, with her muzzle raised to the night sky, she howled and howled. And it wasn't just the dog howling, it was all the dogs she was descended from, clear back to some wolf or other.

She heard footsteps and was sure it was the boy: *He had heard her howling and come from wherever it was he had been all this time and was going to rescue her.* . . .

It turned out to be the man's friend from over the way. He put his lantern on the ground and untied her and talked to her and stroked her ears, and for a minute or two everything was all right. But then she remembered how they didn't tell her to get in the car with them but drove off without even a backward look, and she let out another despairing howl.

Lloyd Wilson tried to get her to go home with him but she couldn't. If she did that, who would be on hand here to guard the property?

In a little while he was back with some scraps for her, which she swallowed so fast that she didn't know afterward what it was she'd eaten. He filled the bowl with water from the pump and left it by the door of her house. Then he called to her and whistled, but she wouldn't budge. "Have it your own way, but I doubt if anybody's going to get a wink of sleep," he said cheerfully, and went off into the darkness.

She howled at intervals all night, and set the other dogs in the neighborhood to barking. The next day when the man's friend came to see how she was getting on, she went halfway to meet him, wagging her behind.

The widow fed her, and the little boys put their arms around her and kissed her on the top of her head, and she felt some better.

That night at supper, with the dog sitting beside his chair and listening as if the story was about her, Lloyd Wilson said, "You never had to tell him anything. When he died, I swore I'd never have another. . . ."

The dog raised her head suddenly. Then she got up and went to the door: a wagon or a cart had turned into the

lane at her place. She whined softly, but nobody paid any
attention until there were footsteps outside and she started
barking. "Be quiet, Trixie," Lloyd Wilson said and pushed
his chair back from the table. In the light from the open
door he saw a young man who looked as if he were about
ready to start running.

"Name's Walker," he said. "I'm your new neighbor. I
told Mr. Smith I'd be here two days ago but my wife took
sick and we had to put off coming. She's still in Mechanics-
burg, where I left her. . . . No thanks, that's very nice of
you. On my way through town I stopped and got something
to eat at the café. You haven't seen anything of my dog,
have you?"

Seeing the rope dangling from the tree, James Walker kept
the dog tied up for the next two days, though he had been
assured it wasn't necessary. But he also fed her and saw that
her pan had water in it and talked to her sometimes. And
when night came there was a light in the kitchen window,
and the dog smelled wood smoke. Things could have been
worse. From time to time she wanted to howl, and managed
not to. The day after that, trucks came, bringing cattle and
hogs and farm machinery and furniture. And that evening
the young man untied the rope and said, "Come on, old girl,
I need you to help me round up the cows." She understood
what he said all right, but she wasn't his old girl, and she
lit off down the road as fast as lightning.

Clarence spent much of the time in his room with the door
closed. He had dark circles under his eyes. His clothes
hung on him. When his mother called him he came to the
table, but throughout the meal he looked at his plate rather
than at them, and they had to ask him two or three times

before he understood that they wanted him to pass something.

His mother tried to get him to see a doctor, but he wouldn't. "There's nothing wrong with my health," he said, in such a way that she was afraid to pursue the matter.

Cletus was sure that his father would come to see them on Christmas morning, bringing presents. Ice skates was what he wanted. A rifle would be even better but you couldn't use it in town, and anyway it would be too expensive. Wayne still believed in Santa Claus. On Christmas Eve, when they undressed, their empty stockings were hanging from the foot of the bed, and they saw by the streetlamp that it was snowing. When they woke up in the morning their stockings were full, and there were more presents waiting for them downstairs. Aunt Jenny had got out her best tablecloth and roasted a capon, and there was a small artificial Christmas tree in the center of the table. They ate till they were stuffed. When they pushed their chairs back, his mother started to clear the table and Aunt Jenny said, "Leave all that till we've had a chance to digest our dinner."

Cletus still wasn't worried. His father had never not given them anything for Christmas.

Wayne wanted to play Old Maid. As Cletus sorted out his cards he listened for the sound of footsteps on the porch. After a while Aunt Jenny got up and began to stir around in the kitchen.

"I find it very strange of your father not to make any effort about your Christmas," Fern Smith said. What she found even stranger was that Cletus didn't seem to care. Maybe it was a stage he was going through, but he seemed so indifferent these days. About everything.

~

The decorated tree on the courthouse lawn was much too large to go in any house. On Christmas Eve people had sung carols around it, but now the square was deserted, except for two men standing in front of the drugstore. One of them was a traveling salesman who hated Christmas. The other was Clarence. Though he was looking straight at the big Christmas tree, he didn't know it was there. Or what day it was. Or why the courthouse square was so deserted.

"I thought the world of him," he said to the traveling salesman, "till he broke up my home. . . ."

Once the dog thought she saw Wayne from a distance, but it turned out to be only another little boy who looked like him. People tried to catch her but she didn't let them get that near. Her coat was dry and her eyes were lackluster and she was skin and bones. She lived on rabbits and other small animals and an occasional chicken that got loose from the run. Finally she ended up in town, where some children chased her and threw sticks at her but she managed to get away from them. At night she foraged in garbage cans.

In the end she found them. Clarence Smith's mother looked out of the window at the side yard and exclaimed, "I declare, it looks like we've got company."

From the way the man made over her, the dog thought she was going to be allowed to stay. And that he would take her to where the boy was. She smiled ingratiatingly at the old woman, who said, "It's all right with me if you want to keep her here," but that wasn't what happened.

In the condition she was in, Clarence couldn't bring himself to give her a beating. He took her back to the farm and said, "I guess you'll have to keep her tied up for a little while. I don't know what's got into her. She's always been a good dog, and never given me any trouble."

Then he went around the place, looking in all the sheds and in the cow barn and the horse barn, for something he'd forgotten or lost somewhere. And a few days later he came back and did the same thing.

The new man's woman came, and more snow fell, and the ground was white, and the snow turned to ice, and the dog slipped and slid when she tried to go anywhere, so she stayed in her house and slept. Sometimes she dreamed she was waiting at the mailbox for the boy to come riding up the road on his bicycle.

Awake she wasn't anybody's dog. When she felt like wandering she waited until the new man wasn't looking and then slipped away.

"The new tenant couldn't get Trixie to stay on the place," Fern said to Cletus. "So your father took her to the vet's and had her put out. With chloroform. You must forgive him. He isn't himself."

She wasn't herself either, or she would have kept this information from him, or at least broken it to him more gently.

Her letters to Lloyd Wilson were now almost entirely taken up with her fears about Clarence.

The lawyer who had successfully steered Fern through the divorce proceedings twiddled his thumbs thoughtfully. Then, leaning back in his chair, he said, "Did Smith actually say in so many words that he was going to shoot you?"

"No," Lloyd Wilson said. "But I know that he has a gun. And from the way he is acting—"

The lawyer glanced at his desk calendar to see what his

next appointment was. "I dare say you have every reason to be alarmed, but unless you can provide a witness who is ready to swear that Smith threatened to take your life, I doubt if the sheriff's office will consider that there are sufficient grounds to issue a warrant for his arrest. Suppose you keep in touch with me, and if there is any change in the situation . . ."

9

The Graduating Class

When I go home, usually because of a funeral, I always end up walking down Ninth Street. I give way to it as if it was a sexual temptation. The house we lived in has changed hands several times, and some fairly recent owner sheared off the whole back part—the pantry, the back stairs, the kitchen, the laundry where the cookstove was, and that upstairs bedroom where the Halloween party took place. Why? To save fuel? The porch railings and the trellises are gone, and so is the low iron fence that separated the front yard from the sidewalk. The high curbing and the two cement hitching posts are still there, having outlived their purpose by half a century. The elm blight killed off the two big trees I played under, and in their place are some storm-damaged maples, so oddly placed that they must have been planted by the birds. In the back yard, where the flower garden used to be, there is a structure about the size and shape of a garage, but with a curtained picture window. Somebody must live in it.

The house next door went up in smoke and flames one night ten or fifteen years ago—defective wiring—and where it stood there is a two-story apartment house that covers half of what used to be our side yard. Here and there all over town big old houses are missing, or between two old houses that have survived somebody has inserted a new house, spoiling my recollection of things. When I come upon the new hospital I totally lose my bearings. Where exactly was the little grocery store my mother used to send me to when she discovered she was out of rice or butter or baking soda? And which wing of the hospital has obliterated the huge bed of violets in the back yard of the house where old Mrs. Harts lived with her son Dave, who never married? And was the bed of violets huge only because the child who once a year knocked on the back door and asked for permission to pick them was so small?

When I dream about Lincoln it is always the way it was in my childhood. Or rather, I dream that it is that way—for the geography has been tampered with and is half real, half a rearrangement of my sleeping mind. For example, the small red-brick house where Miss Lena Moose and Miss Lucy Sheffield lived. It was probably built during the administration of General Ulysses S. Grant, and must have had dark woodwork and heavy curtains shutting out the light. When I dream about it, the proportions are so satisfying to the eye and the rooms so bright, so charming and full of character that I feel I must somehow give up my present life and go live in that house: that nothing else will make me happy. Or I dream that I am standing in front of a house on Eighth Street—a big white house with a corner bay window and carpenter's lace and scalloped siding. I have been brought to a stop there on the sidewalk by the realization that my mother is inside. If I ring the doorbell, she will come and let me in. Or somebody will. And I will go through the house until I find her. But what is she doing there when it is not our house? It doesn't even look like our house. It was built in the eighteen-nineties, and our house is much older than that, and anyway, it's on Ninth Street. In order to deal with this riddle I let my mind wander up Eighth Street, beginning at the corner where the streetcars turn and go downtown, and before I get to the house I was dreaming about I realize there is no such house, and I am, abruptly, awake.

After six months of lying on an analyst's couch—this, too, was a long time ago—I relived that nightly pacing, with my arm around my father's waist. From the living room into the front hall, then, turning, past the grandfather's clock and on into the library, and from the library into the living room. From the library into the dining room, where my mother lay in her coffin. Together we stood looking down at her. I meant to say to the fatherly man who was not my father, the elderly Viennese, another exile, with thick glasses and a Germanic accent, I meant to say *I couldn't bear it*, but what came out of my mouth was "I can't bear it." This statement was followed by a flood of tears such as I hadn't ever known before, not even in my childhood. I got up from the leather couch and, I somehow knew, with his permission left his office and the building and walked down Sixth Avenue to my office. New York City is a place where one can weep on the sidewalk in perfect privacy.

Other children could have borne it, have borne it. My older brother did, somehow. *I* couldn't.

In the Palace at 4 A.M. you walk from one room to the next by going through the walls. You don't need to use the doorways. There is a door, but it is standing open, permanently. If you were to walk through it and didn't like what was on the other side you could turn and come back to the place you started from. What is done can be undone. It is there that I find Cletus Smith.

The little house opposite the fairgrounds looks as if there is nobody there. As if they have gone away on a trip somewhere. Aunt Jenny has pulled the shades to the sill. That way, people won't peer in and see what she sees whenever she closes her eyes, and sometimes when they are wide open. The double bed in the front room is made up and Cletus is lying on it, with his shoes extending over the side so they won't dirty the spread. He is lying on his left side, in the fetal position, as if he is trying to get out of this world by the way he came into it.

The house smells of coffee percolating and then of bacon frying. He does not answer when she tells him breakfast is ready. And neither does he come. Sitting at the kitchen table she blows on her coffee but it is still too hot to drink, so she pours some of it into her saucer. . . . (It is time to let go of all these people and yet I find it difficult. It almost seems that the witness cannot be excused until they are through testifying.)

Aunt Jenny gets up suddenly and goes into the next room and puts her hand on Cletus's forehead. He has no fever but his skin feels clammy and he is very pale. His eyes are open but he doesn't look at her. As she takes her hand away he says, "Would you be afraid if he came here?"

"If who came here?"

He doesn't enlighten her and after a moment she says yes, she would.

"Where do you think he is?"

"I haven't the least iota."

Her hand is not steady enough to drink from the saucer
and so she pours the coffee back into the cup and forgets
to drink it. The clock ticks louder at some times than at
others. She stops hearing it entirely and hears, instead, the
sound of her own heavy breathing. Quarter of nine comes
and she clears her throat and says, "Time you left for school.
You'll be late." He is already late. The clock is five minutes slow, which she knows but has for the moment forgotten. His books are on a chair by the door, but he
knows, even if she doesn't, that he can never go to that
school again. He walks in the Palace at 4 A.M. In that strange
blue light. With his arms outstretched, like an acrobat on
the high wire. And with no net to catch him if he falls.

The meeting in the school corridor, a year and a half later, I
keep reliving in my mind, as if I were going through a series
of reincarnations that end up each time in the same failure. I
saw that he recognized me, and there was no use in my hoping that I would seem not to have recognized him, because I
could feel the expression of surprise on my face. He didn't
speak. I didn't speak. We just kept on walking.

I remember thinking afterward, *When enough time has
passed he will know that I haven't told anybody. . . .* But I
still went on worrying for fear he would think that the
reason I didn't speak to him was that I didn't want to know
him, after what happened. Which is, I'm afraid, what he
did think. What else?

Did he go home and tell his mother? And did they then
pack up and move to another part of Chicago to get away
from me?

If I'd had the presence of mind to say, "You don't have
to worry, I won't tell anybody," would they have been able

to stay where they were? Would his mother have trusted a fifteen-year-old boy to keep such a promise, even if I had made it?

Sometimes I almost remember passing him in the school corridors afterward. And I think, though I am not at all sure of this, that I can remember being happy that I was keeping his secret. Which must mean that he was there, that we continued to pass each other in the halls, that he didn't move away. But if he had stayed on at that school, sooner or later we would have been in the same classroom, and I know that we weren't.

Five or ten years have gone by without my thinking of Cletus at all, and then something reminds me of him—of how we played together on the scaffolding of that half-finished house. And suddenly there he is, coming toward me in the corridor of that enormous high school, and I wince at the memory of how I didn't speak to him. And try to put it out of my mind.

One day last winter, plagued by guilt, I brought down from the attic a grocery carton stuffed with old papers, diplomas, newspaper clippings, letters from college friends I haven't seen for thirty or forty years, and so on, and went through it until I found my high-school yearbook. The photographs of the graduating class are arranged in vertical panels, fifteen oval likenesses to a page. Cletus ought to have been between Beulah Grace Smith and Sophie Sopkin and he isn't. If he had been, I would, I think, have been able to put him out of my mind forever. I went through the yearbook carefully from cover to cover looking for him. He isn't in any group picture or on any list of names.

There is a limit, surely, to what one can demand of one's adolescent self. And to go on feeling guilty about something

that happened so long ago is hardly reasonable. I do feel
guilty, even so. A little. And always will, perhaps, whenever
I think about him. But it isn't only my failure that I think
about. I also wonder about him, about what happened to him.
Whether he was spared the sight of his father's drowned
body. Whether after a while he and his mother were able to
look at each other without embarrassment. Whether he had
as lonely a time as I did when he first moved to Chicago. And
whether the series of events that started with the murder of
Lloyd Wilson—whether all that finally began to seem less
real, more like something he dreamed, so that instead of
being stuck there he could go on and by the grace of God
lead his own life, undestroyed by what was not his doing.